MAGIC IS REAL
PART I.

SEVENTEEN

K.C. MCMILLIAN

NOVELLA

Copyright © 2023 Kiana C. McMillian

KCM Fantasy Fiction

Cover Design: Kiana McMillian

Editor: Caron Pescatore

Mashal High/ Mashalville Logo:

SRIllustrations
3/11/22

Beta Reader: Shalinie Rohit

Print ISBN: 979-8-9878723-0-7

Dedication

I dedicate this to anyone who has struggled with low self-esteem.

Trigger Warnings!

This book contains references to depression, suicide, and murder that some readers may find disturbing. Readers' discretion is advised.

** All spells in this book are a fragment of the Author's imagination and are purely fictional. **

A Special Thanks

Thank you for reading my story and taking a chance on me. I am genuinely grateful to you.
And a special thanks to Shalinie Rohit, Billie Jade Kermack, and Caron Pescatore for all the advice you have given me and for your abundant support on this journey. I love you guys.

To my two boys, mommy loves you so much!
To my husband, Troy McMillian, I love you.

XOXO,

Kiana (K.C.) McMillian

Table of Contents

Chapter 1

Claudette

MY FATHER RECENTLY MARRIED one of the world's worst women, and lucky me, she has twin daughters who are eviler than she is. You know how you eat a peanut butter and jelly sandwich and peel off the ends of the bread because that's something you don't want to eat or be bothered with? Well, yeah, that's what they are, something that should be peeled off and thrown away. Far, far away. Honestly, they are a pain in my neck! It's as if their entire mission in life is to ruin mine, and ever since my father married that dreadful woman, all I have wished for is emancipation. Emancipation is when you divorce your parents, and I have wanted to do it since my father returned from the Islands with her and those twins. But before we get to that, let me introduce myself.

My name is Claudette Richardson. I am sixteen years old, and I will turn the unimportant age of seventeen in two months. I have dark skin, light-brown eyes, a curvy frame, and dark-brown sister locks cascading past my shoulders. Oh, and I am five-three, which many consider short these days. I have two best friends, Spencer, a drama king and always like fifty percent hype, and Nicolette, my calm, laid-back friend. Neither of them treats me differently

1

because I don't have a mother. Spencer is five-ten, handsome, with pale skin and red freckles, while Nicolette has flawless dark skin and a round face. She is slim, is the same height as me, and wears her hair in box braids.

When I was five, my mother died from a heart attack, and my father worked two jobs to keep our house. We lived in a small suburban town with white picket fences, *like in the movies*, and extremely nosey neighbors. Of course, we had an extraordinary golden retriever dog named Buddy, whom I loved so much. I remember how he would greet me and lick my nose when I came home from school, his tongue wet and slimy. I loved it.

Autumn was approaching, the leaves were changing color, and the holiday season was just around the corner. My mom's friend Mirna picked me up from school along with her daughter Sky, which was odd because it was a Thursday, and typically on Thursdays, my mom would pick us up. Mirna seemed nervous or stressed when she arrived, as if she had a lot on her mind. I mean, how do you tell a five-year-old that their mom is dead? I cannot begin to fathom how she must have been feeling.

A dozen police cars surrounded my house, and my father looked devastated as we pulled up. I had no idea what was going on. I ran out of the car down the brick walkway to our home, and I saw the medical examiners walking out with a body covered up that I later found out was my mom. At the time, I didn't exactly know what death meant, but I was sure about to find out.

As my dad sobbed in the bathroom on the day of my mother's funeral, I stood outside the door, covering my ears. I knew that *"death"* was terrible, but come on, I had no idea that when they said my mom was dead, I would never see her again. I remember seeing her beautiful golden-brown face sleeping peacefully, and I thought maybe she was resting. I didn't know I would never see my mommy again.

When my dad finally opened the door, his eyes were puffy and red. My father was tall, about six–one, and had a short fade cut. I remember he looked like he was in his twenties, even though he was in his late thirties then. His skin tone was caramel, and he had a muscular build because of his frequent visits to the gym. According to all my current classmates, my father is an *"old hottie,"* which disgusts me.

After my mom's funeral, my dad took us to Evi's, our favorite ice cream shop. I did not know it then, but that would become one of our rituals on Sundays, Wednesdays, and Fridays.

As the years went on, I realized and better understood what death meant. Whenever I asked my father what had happened to mom, he would disappear into his office for days. Eventually, I gave up asking since it upset him so much. Later, Mirna told me my mom had a heart attack.

We didn't have any other family; my mom was an only child, and her parents died a few years before she met my father and had me. My father was an only child too, who had lost his parents when he was younger. *Note to self: when I find the love of my life, be sure to have at least three kids.*

Back to my point: it's January, and tomorrow we're moving to Mashalville, Long Island. From what I know, it is an imaginary place since I've never heard of it before. However, my stepmom Gabriella wants to move there and begin a new life. Luckily, my father has found a job as an accountant, and his salary can afford to pay for our home. *No more two jobs*!

Gabriella is a clothing designer; she custom-fits middle-class women. She is your go-to if you're attending a dinner party and want to be the best-dressed person. As much as I hate her, I can't deny that she is a talented seamstress. Gabriella has light-brown skin with hazel eyes and curly red hair. She is also curvy; now that I think about it, so was my mom. I guess my dad has a type.

My birthday is two months away, and instead of celebrating my seventeenth birthday with my best friends that I have known all my life, I have to celebrate in a new town, at a new school, around evil step vermin. *Just great.* It's my last day of school, and this woman, *Gabriella*, insisted that the twins and I should go. I would much have preferred to skip the last day and hang out with Nicolette, Spencer, and Mitch.

I check myself out in the mirror. I'm wearing a long black sleeve shirt, with black tights under ripped denim jeans. I have on black suede boots and black leg warmers over my jeans. Black is my favorite color.

"Let's go, girls!" Gabriella screams from the bottom of the stairs. The twins come rushing out of their room, and Marissa bumps into me.

"Get out of my way, freak!" she hisses. Crissy, standing beside her, eyes me warily.

I can't stand Marissa and would turn her into an ant and squash her if I had powers. She is five-nine with light-brown skin, green eyes, and short, purple, and black curly hair. Crissy, her identical twin, has long, black, and green curly hair. They are both attractive and popular at school, and they know it. Sadly, colorism plagues them. They think being light-skinned makes them more attractive than dark-skinned women, and the fact that most of the guys in school chase after them only makes their heads even bigger. *I hope it's not like this at our new school.*

You would think that colorism had died down during this generation, but unfortunately, it hasn't. I can't tell you how often I've been told I was beautiful for a dark-skinned girl. Whatever that means. I roll my eyes and follow the twins downstairs.

SEVENTEEN

Gabriella drives us to school every day. She said we... I mean, *her daughters* are too good to ride the public school bus. Whenever my father is around, Gabriella declares we are queens and should be treated as such. She only includes me in this scenario to present this loving me as one of her own to my dad and everyone else. In truth, Gabriella hates me, and I know she wants to get rid of me by how she treats me.

I'm allergic to peanuts, and she put them in her sweet potato pie last Thanksgiving. I mean, who puts peanuts in sweet potato pie? Is that like a new ingredient? She vowed she didn't know I was allergic, but I'm sure I'd mentioned it before—over ten times! She gave my dad a little twirl, licked her lips, and he was hypnotized. We also had to get rid of Buddy because *she* was allergic.

I sit in the backseat on the right side of the car and rest my head on the window, wishing I were anywhere other than here with people I despise. I plug in my Air Pods, so I can't hear what the idiots are saying and think about when my dad first met Gabriella.

About two years ago, my dad and I were on vacation. We went surfing on the beach, and I was learning new maneuvers I wanted to show him when this woman approached. Seeing her eyeing my dad from a mile away, I watched as she put the moves on him. Mostly, my dad ignored the women who would throw themselves at him, but when I saw his lips curve into a smirk, I knew that was it. The next thing I knew, he was leaving me with my friend Nicolette and her family while he visited Gabriella on the Islands every chance he got. He did it so often that it became infuriating. Once he made it known that he and Gabriella were dating, all the other women in the PTA were disappointed, and the free meals they usually plied him with abruptly stopped. The first time I met the twins, Marissa spat her gum in my hair, and my dad had to cut my hair shorter because it wouldn't come out.

Gabriella said Marissa suffered from anxiety, so she acted "*nervously*" when we met. *What did that have to do with her spitting gum into my hair?* I wondered. Eventually, I decided just to let my hair lock up.

Crissy is creepy; she doesn't speak and follows Marissa everywhere like a shadow. They have this weird twin bond thing. Honestly, I don't understand it, but I am an only child. Either way, I don't like them. They are bullies and pick on me, my friends, and other kids. This one time, they bullied this girl so badly that she stopped coming to school. The next thing I knew, she was dead, and her mom and dad moved away. I am pretty sure she committed suicide because I overheard a few parents whispering about a note she had left. *Either that or the twins murdered her.* I was sure the twins had something to do with her disappearance.

When we arrive at the school, Gabriella kisses Crissy and Marissa on the cheek and tells them she loves them. Times like this make me wish my mother were alive. I walk away swiftly to find my friends.

Walking down the hallway, I take in the scent. It smells like a sweaty wrestler. I glance around at my classmates; some I will miss, and some I absolutely will not. I will miss the nice kids, the small conversations I usually have with some of my peers before classes begin, and the terrible sloppy joe sandwiches the lunch ladies make. And I will definitely miss Mr. Edwards! I hate math, but wow, he makes suffering through that class worth it. When he turns to face the board, we can see his firm butt. Oh my! I love watching him solve for X because he goes slow, and all the girls, including myself, watch how he moves his arms on that whiteboard, flexing his muscles. I was in lust. Man, I wish I were that board whenever he used scented markers and would lean in to smell them. But thinking about it now, that is a pretty weird thing to do because who leans into a whiteboard and smells the marker scent? Getting flustered from thinking about Mr. Edwards, I lean against the locker, close my eyes, and take in the aroma—a little tear forms at the corner of my eye. I have been living here all my life and will genuinely miss it.

Chapter 2

Last Day

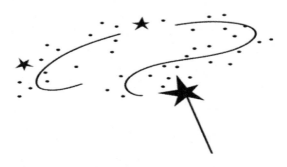

TEARS FALL DOWN my face, and I am full-on crying. I don't want to leave my home and start over again, especially in the middle of the school year. What would make my father accept a new job offer now?

"Move it, Blacky! You're in my way," Marissa screeches, shoving me aside.

Okay, granted, I was standing in front of her locker, but was there a need to shove me? Let alone call me Blacky? Technically, I am dark brown; I am not black. Black is a color, but again, *whatever*. I do not say a word; I just let her shove me. I know if I retaliate, her shadow will get involved, and although we were leaving this school, I am sure she would send her minions after me.

I motion toward her locker as if she is a Queen, and I am clearing the way. She gives me a sadistic smirk, and I walk to Spencer's locker to wait for him to arrive at school. Classes start at nine, but we have homeroom for fifteen minutes, and I usually walk with him and his boyfriend, Mitch.

Mitch and Spencer have been together for two years and are each other's first. When they came out, it was the talk of the school, and kids bullied them for it, but Nicolette and I stood our ground and continued being his friend. Which ultimately resulted in our demise. We were once popular, but when we did not participate in bullying Spencer, that was it for us. I was not into that; I love everyone who loves me back. I do not believe in bullying someone just because they are different. We will be friends if you are an incredible person and we vibe. I do not care about race, religion, or sexual preferences. But the people I go to school with are dissatisfied with themselves, and they take it out on others.

"Hey, Claudette, what's up?" Spencer grins as he approaches.

I groan. "Do you really need to ask?"

"What did the demon twins do to you now?" He shakes his head, sighing.

"The usual." My voice is flat.

"They're unhappy with themselves and insecure about their looks and skin color. That is the only reason they make fun of you."

I am confused by his statement. "Everyone thinks they are the most beautiful girls in school. Why would they be insecure?"

"Everyone is insecure about something, Claudette." He wraps his arm around me as we head toward homeroom.

"Hey, Spence?" I look up at him.

"Yeah?"

"Where's Mitch?" Those two are never apart.

Spencer frowns. "He sends his apologies. He's out sick, so he will miss your last day."

"Oh, aw, that sucks! I was looking forward to seeing him today." I pout. "But I hope he gets better soon." Mitch is hilarious; he is the one I go to when I feel down. He is an excellent match for Spencer.

We walk into the classroom; Mr. George is writing his plan for the history class on the chalkboard. We listen to the school announcements, say the pledge of allegiance, and then it is time to start the day.

By the fourth period, I am exhausted from smiling and engaging with everyone. My teachers decided that today would be the day they focused on the fact that I was leaving. Any other day they did not care that the girl with no mom existed, but oh, because today is my last day, let us make a spectacle out of it.

Fourth period I have math, and I can't wait! I saw Mr. Edwards during the second period, and he wore those slim-fit dress pants that curved his butt in the right way. He has what I describe as "a firm, perky bootie" that sits up effortlessly. I am obsessed with my high school math teacher, which is terrible, but it's an innocent crush. I know nothing would ever come from it, but I hope to find an eye candy nearly as hot as him when I get to my new school.

"Hello, class." Mr. Edwards claps his hands to get our attention. "Please take your seats."

I always sit right in front to have the perfect view of him.

"Claudette, today is your last day with us. How are you feeling?" he asks in his husky tone. *Oh no! Not again.* I want to become invisible. I am so tired of answering that question. I would have skipped classes today if I had known this would be such a huge deal.

"I am feeling okay; thank you for asking, Mr. Edwards," I reply.

"Glad to hear it." He claps his hands again, then turns to write on the chalkboard. "Okay, students." Mr. Edwards pivots his attention back to the class. "Today, we will go more in-depth with the quadratic formula; please pay attention!"

The rest of that math lesson is a blur to me. Mr. Edwards sounds like he is saying, "blah, blah, blah." I am too distracted gazing at him instead of listening to what he is saying. So embarrassing! I am unsure how far along my new math class is, so perhaps I should have paid more attention to what he was teaching us rather than staring at him.

After the bell rings, I run out of the classroom so quickly you would have thought smoke was trailing me. I head down the hallway to my locker to put my books away. It is my lunch period; thankfully, I have lunch with Nicolette and Spencer. Spencer has lunch during the sixth period, but because this is his free period, he eats with us and goes to the library during his actual lunch period.

In our school, everyone is part of a clique. You have the cool kids, who are the ones who have wealthy or very successful parents and don't want to attend private school. You have the intelligent kids; all classes they take are AP. You have the jocks comprising basketball, soccer, football, and tennis players. Parents and the school district fought over separate teams because male and female basketball, soccer, and tennis players could not play together. Parents wanted a female football team, and the school board compromised and settled for girls' flag football instead. They take up two long tables in the middle of the lunchroom because there are so many of them. Of course, you have the cheerleaders who sit with the jocks. You have the nerds, which you would think would be the smart kids, but in my school, the nerds are the goofy individuals who are only good at math and science. There are the awkward kids who drink, smoke cigarettes and weed, and wear black clothes. And then there are us, *"the outcasts."* Which means we used to be a part of a clique but got kicked out. It is ridiculous.

Nicolette and I head to the lunch line to grab our food. Today is sloppy joe Thursday, and for dessert, they are giving away mini cheesecakes thanks to Trina, the lunch lady. One day each week, she makes a special dessert and brings it for us to try. She plans to start a "Trina's Sweet Treats Dessert Truck" and uses us as her tasters, I had no complaints because everything she makes is delicious.

Our table is the rocky one no one wants, which is by the water fountains. Five people can fit at this table instead of ten to fifteen.

"Hey guys," Spencer says as he sits beside Nicolette.

"Hey, Spence." Nicolette nudges him with her shoulder. "Where is your other half?" She takes a bite of her cheesecake.

"He is not feeling well today."

"Oh, no!" Nicolette's eyes widen.

While Nicolette and Spencer chat, I devour my food as quickly as possible. I have to meet with my guidance counselor, Ms. Cameau, to discuss my progress and all the information they need to transfer to my new school.

Besides my friends, Ms. Cameau is the *only* other person in the school that I feel comfortable speaking with. She has light-brown skin, bright red hair, brown eyes, and is short, like me. She is also awkward but in a great funny way.

"Hey, guys, I'm going to head to Ms. Cameau's office now. I'll catch up with you two after school."

My friends nod in acknowledgment, still deep in conversation, and I get up and head toward the door to exit the lunchroom.

In the office, I spot Ms. Cameau struggling with her office door. When our gazes meet, she drops the papers she is carrying.

"Would you like me to help you with those?" I say.

"No honey, I got it. Thank you, though. Come on in." She ushers me into her office, quickly picking up the papers from the floor.

I walk in and sit down. Ms. Cameau's favorite color is purple, so everything in her office, besides the desk and chairs, is some shade of that color.

"Have a seat." Ms. Cameau moves to sit behind her desk.

I sit in the brown chair, glancing around her office and smiling. I am going to miss coming here and having our chats. I came here because I needed help to grieve my mother's death and deal with my day-to-day high school life, but I have come to think of Ms. Cameau as a friend.

"How are you feeling today?" She tilts her head and stares at me with genuine interest.

"I am not okay."

She nods and scribbles on her lavender notepad. "Would you like to tell me about it?" Ms. Cameau weighs her luck in getting me to talk more about it.

"Not really," I say deadpan.

"Okay, so what would you like to talk about?"

"I don't know. Do you have anything to talk about?" I look everywhere in the room but at her.

"Well, I have recommended to your father a therapist for you. I believe you would benefit from it."

"What? Where is this therapist located?"

"She is in your new town, which is not far from here. I found three potential therapists, and this one insisted on meeting you. Of course, you can always reach out to me," she says.

I laugh. Here I have been acting like I was moving out of the state and only moving a few towns over. "Yes! That would be great!" I am sure whoever the woman Ms. Cameau recommended has to be just as great as her. Unfortunately, my new school doesn't have guidance counselors; I am unsure why.

"So, how are you feeling about moving away?" Ms. Cameau asks.

"I am not okay with it." I huff. "For one thing, I don't particularly care for my stepmother or her children. For another, we are moving to a new town they chose, which seems like a setup."

She scribbles in her notepad and nods. "I see. What would you say is the issue with your stepmother? From an outsider's perspective, she appears to care about you."

That's what she wants all of you fools to believe! I fidget in my seat.

I don't like it when people, especially Ms. Cameau, state the obvious. It seems like Gabriella cares about me, but I know she does not. It was just a matter of proving it to others. But she is so on point with her acting skills I can never catch her slipping. Only my friends believe me.

"Well?" she says, waiting for my response.

Pressing my lips together, I fold my arms. "I don't trust her!"

"I see. And why don't you trust her?"

At that moment, I am so ready for this session to be over. I glance at the clock and see we still have fifteen minutes to go. I decide to change the subject. "How many days will I have to meet with this therapist?" I ask instead of answering her irrelevant question.

Ms. Cameau makes another note in her notepad, giving me a warm smile. "How about we end now since you arrived earlier? I will call your father on Monday to discuss this with him."

"Excellent." I grab my belongings, and we embrace before I hasten out of her office.

The rest of the day goes by in the blink of an eye, and the next thing I know, I am in the car with the demon twins and their evil mother. Spencer and Nicolette arrive to see me off as soon as we get home. Everything is packed, and mommy dearest will cook dinner for us once we arrive at the new house.

"I'm going to miss you so much, Claudette!" Nicolette gives me a bear hug.

"Me too, and I know Mitch will as well!" Spencer cries, joining in on the group hug.

"We will be there for your birthday!" Nicolette blinks back tears.

"I will miss you guys too, and you better be there!" I say, teary-eyed.

"Of course, I already spoke to my mom, and she talked to

Spencer's mom. They plan to bring us out there, although we have been trying to find your new town on Google maps, and we can't." Nicolette says.

"That's very odd; perhaps I'll come to you guys instead," I suggest.

"What's your address again?" Spencer asks.

"1103 TK Avenue."

Spencer types the address into his phone, and nothing comes up.

I spot my dad walking toward the car with the rest of our things and decide to ask him about it. "Hey, dad, what is the address of our new home? We can't seem to find it on Google."

"The address is 1103 TK Avenue," he says, showing me the location on his phone. It is peculiar; I can see it on his phone but not on mine or anyone else's.

"Okay, Claudette, say goodbye to your friends. We must head out now because you and the twins are starting your new school tomorrow," Gabriella's voice annoyingly echoes.

Tomorrow is Friday. Who starts a new school on a Friday?

"Who starts a new school on a Friday? That doesn't make any sense," Nicolette whispers, imitating my exact thoughts.

The fact that we think alike is one reason I love her. I smile and hug her one last time. Mommy dearest gives my friends a fake smile while the twins scowl at us as they walk toward the car. Spencer hugs me, and my eyes fill with tears.

I sit inside the car, buckle my seatbelt, and turn around to see my best friends waving at me through the back window. My dad starts the car and drives forward, and I stare out the window at my friends until they are no longer visible. I am going to miss them terribly.

Welcome To

MASHALVILLE

Chapter 3

New Girl

I AM GETTING ready to head to my new school, Mashal High, and dreading the first day. To make matters worse, we must wear uniforms. *Who wears uniforms in a public school?* Burgundy, gold, and black are the school colors. Females must wear burgundy, black, and gold plaid skirts with thick black stockings and burgundy button-up long-sleeve shirts with this strange Sun, Moon, and Earth logo. It is odd because when we first entered the town, there was a sign that said, "Welcome to Mashalville," with the same Sun, Moon, and Earth symbol. *What is with this town and that symbol?*

I finish getting dressed, place my locks into a bun, and head down the spiral stairs to await the demon twins and mommy dearest. My dad had already gone to work and told me he would be late for dinner. I felt utterly alone. My dad and I used to do everything together, but since he married Gabriella, we have no alone time. I cannot remember the last time we went to Evi's for ice cream.

"Are you girls ready for your first day?" Gabriella asks as she walks to the closet and grabs her car keys and purse.

"Yes, Mom!" Marissa drags her feet as she walks from the kitchen with a raisin muffin, Crissy hovering behind her.

When we arrive at the school, I am stunned; it looks like a miniature castle from a movie. The architecture combines ancient and modern, and a gold sign with the Sun, Moon, and Earth symbol hangs over the school's entrance.

"Have a great day, girls," Gabriella squeals before she speeds away.

I glance at Marissa and Crissy, noticing they seem nervous. In our previous school, they always exhibited confidence, so how should I feel if they are worried now? As we walk through the doors, a weird gray smoke circles us, and I cannot breathe for a few seconds. *What is happening?* I cough uncontrollably. The twins look worried about me for a change, yet they are not coughing like I am.

"Hey there, are you okay?" a strange girl standing behind me asks.

"Yeah, I think so. What was that?" I respond in a strained voice.

"Oh, I am not sure how to answer that," she says.

Um, what? What does she mean she's not sure how to answer that?

"What?" I frown. "What was the smoke for?"

"Calm down; the smoke is our way of checking for weapons," a tall, pale-faced man explains. "Hello, I am principal Deanwall. Nice to meet you."

"Nice to meet you, too." Marissa shakes his hand.

"You have a firm handshake, young lady! Follow me. I will show you to your escorts." Principal Deanwall turns and starts walking away.

Escorts? What type of school is this?

All eyes are on us as we walk by. I feel like a fish in a bowl, or worse, like a fish out of water, grappling for air.

The girls look amazing in their uniforms, while the boys have me tripping over my feet. Almost every guy is attractive, wearing fitted khaki pants and burgundy button-up shirts. Suddenly, I notice a tall, green-eyed, muscular god staring at me. He must be at least six foot one. When our gazes meet, he smirks, and my jaw drops. *Is it hot in here?* In response to his gaze, Marissa rolls her eyes at me. I can feel her jealousy radiating at me.

"Please take a seat; your escorts will be with you shortly," Principal Deanwall says once we arrive at his office.

"Are we each getting our own escort?" Marissa asks.

"Yes, you are all three separate individuals who require three escorts," he answers matter-of-factly.

"My sister and I do everything together, so we only need one escort. Thank you." Marissa's tone is firm.

"I'm sorry. Did I give you the impression that you had a choice? You will each have your own. Whatever crap you pulled at your old school will not work here," Principal Deanwall says, dismissing her request as he hurries away.

Marissa stands there with an annoyed expression, shocked that, for once, she has not gotten her way. The little princess is not used to that, and I try my hardest not to laugh. After a moment, three individuals enter the office. The twins and I are speechless when we notice the sexy god from the hallway. He walks in with one female and another less attractive male. *Please let that sexy one be my escort!*

"Hi, my name is Kevin Evans. Nice to meet you all," the sexy god says in a deep, husky voice, making me want to melt. I peek at the twins, probably convulsing in their pants, just like me.

"Which one of you is Claudette?" He flashes a sexy smile, glancing at his clipboard. This is the one time I have ever been super excited that my name is Claudette. I raise my hand, moving closer to him. I can see the twins' death glares out of the corner of my eye.

"Follow me." He flashes me another spine-tingling smile.

"With pleasure," I whisper, licking my lips and winking at Marissa.

"What was that?" Kevin asks.

"I said sure." I bite my lip, hoping he hadn't seen the wink.

Kevin and I leave the office and walk down an old hallway that needs renovation. I do not see any other students, so I assume they are already in class. Kevin stops in front of a locker and puts in his combination; I stand, shuffling my feet, waiting for him to say something. I swear I am lusting over him because he is so fine. He is a mouth-watering sight to see. I am completely enamored with him. *Pull yourself together, girl!* My inner voice, which I like to call Detta, is clamoring.

He rests his tall, slender body against his locker. "So let me explain this school to you." I do not know if he has a six-pack or eight under that button-up shirt, but I know I would not mind exploring more. He reaches into his pocket and grabs a pen, flexing his muscles. *He is doing this on purpose!*

"Our school is divided into two wings—East and West. This wing we are in now is the East; after your seventeenth birthday, you will understand the significance of this wing compared to the West."

I have no idea what this beautiful man is talking about, but I listen intently. After the silence between us stretches for a few seconds, it clicks.

"Wait! I'm sorry, what does my seventeenth birthday have to do with anything?" I furrow my brow.

"My apologies, Claudette, but I can't reveal that to you until then," Kevin says.

"I don't understand."

"I will explain that to you after your birthday."

"How old are you?" I ask him.

"I'm seventeen." His full lips curve into yet another sexy smile.

"I thought you were supposed to be my escort. Doesn't that mean you should explain everything to me?" I challenge him, but internally, I am swooning over his smile.

"The only thing I can tell you, for now, is that all your classes are in the East Wing. After your seventeenth birthday, you will have a decision to make. That is when you will stay in the East Wing or move to the West. I'm sorry, but I can't say anymore. But I can show you where all your classes are. Students from the East and West wings only interact during lunch and gym periods."

"You are being very vague, sir, but okay." I shrug.

He licks his lips sensually, making me bite back a groan, and I nearly faint when he grasps my hand. I am confused. He is incredibly charming, but I do not understand why he is holding my hand. He must have noticed my facial expression because he lets go immediately. I glance down at his hand and mine, then look into his beautiful green eyes.

"I'm sorry. I should have asked if I could touch you," he says.

You can do whatever you want to me. I blush. "It's no worries. Lead the way."

"The hallway is very slippery sometimes, so watch your step," he advises.

I follow him down the dark hallway and listen while he tells me about the teachers, the classes they teach, which ones he thinks are cool, and the ones he does not like. What I really want to know is if he is single. At my other school, all the guys were duds, and I could not connect with any of them. I want someone I can spend most of my time with; I am still a virgin, but despite my non-existent sex life, my sex drive is extremely high. That makes little sense, but Nicolette would always say that whenever I was attracted to some guy. Spencer and Nicolette are not virgins, but they always tell me I should wait until I find someone with whom I have a genuine connection. I know absolutely nothing about Kevin, but one thing I know for sure is that I want him.

I trail Kevin to my first class, which he also has. English is my favorite subject, so it is my only advanced class. I look at him as he opens the door and ushers me inside. All eyes are on me as I enter the room, and I feel very exposed. I don't like it. At that moment, I wished I was stranded somewhere in a desert, swallowed whole by quicksand.

"Ms. Richardson, nice to meet you," a loud, deep voice says from behind me. I look at the sizable frumpy man and smile.

"Please take a seat," he says.

I sit next to Kevin. Apparently, when you are assigned an escort and have the same class as them, the other kids automatically have to leave two spots open. *Go figure.*

"My name is Mr. Rogers. Please review our syllabus and let me know if there are any books you haven't read."

I skim over the syllabus, and from what I can tell, I have read all the books listed. I smile and inform Mr. Rogers that I have read them. In return, he announces that we have a pop quiz, and by the looks on everyone's faces, it seems as if it is my fault. *Oops!*

Each class is supposed to last about thirty-five minutes, but it seems to take the bell forever to ring, and when it does, it is different. It is a *ding, ding, boom,* which sounds like an off-key tune I can't quite catch. Kevin takes my books and insists on showing me to my next class.

"Are you going to show me to all my classes?" I peer at his handsome face from beneath my lashes.

"Yes. I am your escort, so I have to *escort* you to all your classes for the day." Kevin winks.

"And how long are you supposed to do this for?" I cock my head and look at him, trying not to stare at those full lips.

"We're only obligated to do it for a week, and then you're on your own."

"What made you sign up to be my escort?" I ask, unsure I want to know the answer. Suppose he is just being nice to me, and we have no connection!

"I didn't sign up to be *your* escort. I signed up as *an* escort, and the principal assigned you to me."

My face flushes a bright red, and I gaze at my feet. *Duh, Claudette. Obviously, he did not sign up to be* your *escort. Where is that quicksand when you need it?*

"Here is your history class. We only have English, gym, and lunch together. I will see you after history to take you to your next class." Kevin hands me my books and walks away. I take a deep breath and enter the classroom. It is a small class; there must be about ten students here, and they are all chit-chatting. My entering does not stop the conversation. I spot a desk in the back corner and sit there. I take out my phone and send Nicolette and Spencer a text message, telling them I miss them, and quickly snap a sad-faced picture of myself as proof. The weird off-key bell rings, and the teacher walks in. She begins to write on the chalkboard without looking in my direction, not even bothering to introduce herself to me.

When that class ends, I am ready to see Kevin again; he is so hot. The next class is science, which is pretty quick as today they are taking a test on the homework given to them yesterday. Since today is my first day, I just read the previous chapter. Lunch is next, and Kevin meets me at my science class. While walking to the cafeteria, we pass through the West Wing, and I cannot help noticing the twins and their escorts. The twins are already seventeen, so I assume that is why they are in the West Wing. But then again, Kevin is also seventeen. *This school is strange.*

"Hey, so everyone has a specific place where they sit," Kevin says, breaking into my reverie.

If it is anything like my previous school, I already know that the popular kids sit on one side, and then you have all the other groups. Although, by the looks of this cafeteria, it seems much worse.

All West Wing students sit on the left, and the East Wing sits on the right.

"Never cross paths with the students on the left. They will destroy you!" Kevin looks at me, his eyes fierce.

Huh? I am unsure how I am supposed to take that; this school is full of teenagers; how much destruction can they do? Without saying a word, I nod.

"I don't always eat lunch here; I am going to my car today. Would you like to join me?" Kevin offers.

Woah! My knees feel weak, like Jell-O. Of course, I want to join him, but we just met, so it is not a smart idea. He looks me in the eye when the silence lingers between us for more than a few uncomfortable seconds. "It's okay, Claudette, you can say no."

"Maybe, another time," I murmur. Kevin nods, grabs his food, and heads out of the cafeteria. I look around, trying to determine where I should or could sit. I get my food, which I have to say is a better selection than at my old school.

There are sandwiches like actual cold cuts that look scrumptious, potato salad, all selections of salads, and peanut butter and jelly. *Wow!* What lunchroom serves potato salad? I take one and head to the outside court. Few students are out here, and I have no idea which side is West versus East, so I sit in the middle, looking around to ensure I am not breaking some obscene rule.

Feeling lonely, I take out my phone and text Nicolette and

Spencer in our group chat.

 Me: Guys, I hate it here! ☹

 Spencer: How bad is it?

 Nicolette: Not that many hot guys, huh?

 Me: Actually, there are a lot of hot guys here. And one of them is my escort.

 Spencer: ESCORT? What kind of freaky school is this?

 Nicolette: My thoughts exactly!

I cannot stand my friends; they always have to be extra. When I am about to respond, I notice a young olive-toned girl with curly hair standing in the window a few stories above me. She looks like she is under the influence. *Oh my God! She is about to jump!*

I run inside screaming, "She is going to jump! She is going to jump!" No one so much as budges. I do not know where the girl is or on what floor. I focus on how many windows up I saw her. It's the fifth window. That means it has to be on the fifth floor. I run down the hallway, searching and praying that I am not too late. I finally reach the bathroom where she is. She is standing on the ledge outside the window; her face is wet from tears, and streaks of black eye makeup run down her cheeks. *What could have happened to her to make her want to jump?*

"Hello... Why are you standing outside the window?" I try to make small talk with her.

"Don't come any closer!" she bellows.

"Okay, I am not." I raise my hands at my side, palms facing forward as though in surrender. "I am going to stand right here. My name is Claudette. I am new here; what's your name?"

She glances at me but does not say a word. When her focus is no longer on me, I move closer. I carefully place one foot in front of the other, trying to be as quiet as possible.

"Trust me. You don't want to be in this school! It's full of evil witches!" she hisses.

"I am sure all schools have evil witches; it doesn't mean you have to jump to be rid of them." I do not know what she means by witches. She can't be serious.

"No! You don't understand." She frowns at me.

"Well, how about you come back inside and explain it to me? I am having a hard time fitting in," I say, trying to reason with her.

"How can I trust you're not like everyone else here?" she asks. I can see the pain in her eyes as she questions my intentions.

"It's hard trusting someone. I don't believe I am like everyone else, but that's something for you to determine. You will only know if you come back inside. This is not the way. Trust me, *I know.* I have been where you are," I confide. "I wanted to end my life; I wanted the pain to be over. But believe me when I say someone needs you."

She turns to face me, steps back inside the window, and falls into my arms, sobbing. I know how she feels. A little after my father married that woman, I felt overwhelmed and alone. I wanted to die, so I took pills and hoped for the best. Fortunately, I didn't take enough; they only made me extremely sick. That was why I started seeing Ms. Cameau five days a week instead of the original two days. They even discussed whether I should see a therapist outside school, but I told my dad it was unnecessary. He agreed and repeatedly told me how much he loved me and did not want to lose me. I felt terrible, but sadly, that was not the only time I attempted suicide.

"What's your name?" I ask warily, wondering if she will tell me.

She lets me go and wipes her eyes. "Isabel Garcia." Her voice is low and husky.

"Nice to meet you, Isabel."

She gives me a soft smile and regards me with beautiful green-blue eyes. She has honey-blonde curls, thin eyebrows, a round face, and a curvy body. I do not know what would make her want to end her life, but I know it has something to do with this weird school.

"Today is my seventeenth birthday." Her Spanish accent shines through.

"Oh, happy birthday, Isabel." I smile.

"It's not a happy day because I have an important decision to make," she says, and my smile falters.

"I am sure whatever decision you have to make shouldn't make you want to end your life."

"How old are you, Claudette?" Isabel eyes me curiously.

"I am sixteen." *What is this town's obsession with my age?*

She backs away from me slowly, frowning.

Her response and the change in her energy bewilder me. *What did I do? What did I say?* "What is it?"

"Oh, mama! You're sixteen; when do you turn seventeen?"

"My birthday is March twentieth. I don't understand. Why do you look so worried?" I push for answers.

"I'm sorry, Claudette, but I can't tell you. You will know once you turn seventeen. I have already said too much." Isabel gives me the same vague response Kevin had.

When I am about to say something else, a girl bursts into the bathroom with other students. They ignore me and escort Isabel out, asking her if she has revealed anything to me. She tells them she did not.

What am I missing? I am so confused, but before I can dwell on it anymore, the bell rings, and it is time for my next class.

Chapter 4

Fitting in With the Cool Kids

THE REST OF the day is a blur. I can't wait to be home in bed and away from this eerie school. The weekend has arrived, and I want to read over some class assignments to prepare for Monday. My thoughts turn to Kevin, how sexy he is, and how he invited me to have lunch in his car. *Has he asked other girls, or is it just me?* But then again, there is no reason for me to feel special. Suddenly my phone beeps, notifying me of a text message from an unknown number.

Unknown: Hi, this is Kevin. I got your number from the system.

Woah! Stalker much? But I couldn't lie; it was as if I manifested it to happen. I was smiling from ear to ear. After smiling for way too long, I reply.

Me: Number saved.

I didn't know how to respond. I want to seem cool and not extremely thirsty because, trust me, my mouth is watering.

Kevin: Are you busy today?

For you, handsome, I am never busy.
Me: Not really. Why? What's up?
Smooth.
Kevin: Would you like to meet at the park later? I am meeting a few friends and wondered if you would like to join us.

As much as I want to join, I know it isn't a good idea, and I also know that my dad will not allow me to go, even if other people are around. My father doesn't have a problem with me dating. He just wants to have dinner with the guy beforehand, get to know him, and embarrass me a little. I just met Kevin and am unsure if he is attracted to me or only wants to be friends. I must get to know him better and see if the feeling is mutual before putting myself through the embarrassment with my dad.

Me: Maybe that's not a good idea.
Kevin: Understood. I will see you at school on Monday.

I throw my phone aside, turn onto my belly, and plunge my face into my pillow, belting out a small scream. I seriously have a crush on a guy I just met, and I have no idea if he feels the same. A knock at the door distracts me from my lusting for Kevin.

"You can come in," I shout.

My father walks in with a stern expression.

I roll over and sit up, biting my lip. "What is it, dad?"

"Ms. Cameau called me yesterday and suggested you see a therapist. Is everything okay with you? Please let me know if you feel overwhelmed, like when we were back home. I love you and need you in this world. Please don't do anything to hurt yourself again. I know the move—"

"Dad, I'm fine. I don't intend to hurt myself; I understand that suicide is not the way. But I should speak to a therapist. I feel a little overwhelmed with this new school and have a lot to sort out." I give him a reassuring smile.

"Honey, I am sorry we had to move, but there is something that you will find out once you turn seventeen. Just know that I am always here for you."

"Okay! What is it, dad? Seventeen is not an important age, yet you and everyone in this weird town have been making such a huge deal! What am I missing about the significance of turning seventeen?" I cross my arms, pressing my lips together.

"I am sorry, honey, but I can't tell you that." He looks away briefly, and then our gazes meet. "Trust me when I say it will all make sense on your birthday. This town is my home, and although I left, I decided it was best to move back so that you could make a vital decision on your own."

"Dad, what are you talking about?" I scrunch up my face. "What decision do I have to make?" I question for what seems like the millionth time since moving here.

"When the time comes, you will know." His response is vague, like everyone else's.

"Dad, you are being so vague and creepy, but okay." My shoulders sag. I already feel exhausted from this topic.

"I love you, Cheetah!" My father kisses me on the cheek. He calls me a cheetah because it's my favorite animal.

"I love you too, Dad," I reply.

"Okay, get out and meet some new people. Don't stay cooped up in this room all weekend. But you know the deal with boys. They must have dinner with the family before you spend time with them alone!" he instructs in a fatherly tone.

I roll my eyes. "Perhaps I will work on that next weekend. Since you and Gabriella had the genius idea of moving in the middle of the school year."

"Okay, I will let you have that one," he says, snickering as he closes the door behind him.

33

I find it weird that he would tell me I have some decision to make when I turn seventeen. *What decision?*

I spend the rest of the weekend alone in my room, wanting to stay away from Gabriella and the twins. Scrolling through Instagram, I search for Kevin, Isabel, and a few other names of people at my new school. I find them but don't want to follow them immediately. Luckily, their pages are public, so I can stalk them for a while first.

I look over Isabel's feed. She seemed pretty happy until her parents were murdered recently, right before her seventeenth birthday. So far, they have not caught the killers. *No wonder she wants to commit suicide.* Her recent posts are about how much she misses them and wants to join them. Isabel turned her comments off, except for one post of her and her mother. People have been giving their condolences. And her last post is of a prayer in Spanish with a lengthy caption, displaying her hurt about no longer having a family. I like all three posts and follow her, hoping she will follow me back if or when she signs back into Instagram.

I check out Kevin's page next, and from what I can tell from his posts, he isn't close with his parents; he has two friends–Tanya and Tristan–and there is no sign of a girlfriend. I smile.

After stalking Kevin's and Isabel's pages, I head to bed. It is Sunday, and tomorrow is school. I look forward to seeing Kevin and hopefully building a friendship with Isabel.

I wake up early Monday morning, shower, style my locks into a bun, and dress in my Mashal High uniform. It is pretty warm today, so I don't have to wear thick black stockings with my skirt. Not saying a word to the twins or Gabriella, I hop into the car and wait for them to come so we can head to school. But when they get in, they don't say anything to me, which is odd. Usually, Marissa has some sly comment, and Gabriella says something irrelevant. But today, they say nothing.

Once we arrive at school, I decide to try to fit in with the students on the east side. I head to my locker to get my books for my first-period class when I see Kevin approaching.

"Hey Claudette, how was your weekend?" He grins.

"It was pretty good, and yours?" I smile back, feeling butterflies from seeing him.

"It was smooth. Want to hang out after school?" He waggles his eyebrows.

"Um..." I stand frozen, not believing all I have to say is, *um.* Of course, I want to hang out with him, but all I can think of is my father's reaction.

"What is it?" he asks, his eyes concerned.

"So, my father disapproves of me spending time with, you know, boys unless he meets them first, even if it's just as friends," I explain, as I feel my cheeks growing hot.

I added the friend part because, to be honest, I still do not know if Kevin is attracted to me.

He leans closer, and I can feel his warm, minty breath on my face. In a husky tone, he says, "I would not let my daughter leave my sight if she were as beautiful as you."

Um... I'm sorry. What? Did he just say I was beautiful? I swear I am melting, and my underwear feels damp.

"I wouldn't mind meeting your dad. Just let me know when and where." A panty-melting smile traces his very edible lips.

I gulp. "Actually, what I need to know is—"

"I am interested in being more than just friends," he says, cutting me off.

I blink. "I'm sorry. What?" *Did he say what I think he said?*

"I am interested in you, Claudette. It is purely physical because I don't know much about you, but I am interested in getting to

35

know you. And if one requirement of making that happen is meeting your father, then so be it."

I gape at him, not knowing what to say.

This beautiful guy is interested in me, *little old me*. He pulls out his phone, asks for my socials, and follows me. The sound of the bell forces us to break apart, and we head to our classes.

Soon it is lunchtime, and I look forward to seeing Kevin again. This time, I want to eat lunch with him in his car. Although I tell myself I am okay with not fitting in, a voice inside me calls me a liar.

I go to the lunchroom, intent on finding Kevin, but when I don't see him immediately, I sigh and grab a salad. I survey the cafeteria again for him but still don't see him. As I am about to leave, someone seizes my hand. It is Kevin!

"Would you like to sit outside?" he asks.

I nod, and we head outside to sit on the East Side of the courtyard.

"So, this is the side we're supposed to sit on?" I ask.

"Yes, it is. You will understand–"

"More when I turn seventeen. Yeah, yeah, yeah," I say, cutting him off.

"Don't be rude." He takes a bite of his chicken sandwich. Even the way he chews his food is sexy. *Like, does this guy know what he is doing to me?*

"Kevin, I don't understand. What is so special about turning seventeen?"

"I wish I could explain it. I can only imagine how you must feel. But unfortunately, I can't. It's against the rules." He sighs.

"The rules?" I raise an eyebrow.

"Yes, the rules of this town. Turning seventeen is significant here in Mashalville, and you will better understand once you have reached the age," Kevin explains without telling me anything.

I don't know what to say to that. I am so frustrated about this age thing that I don't say another word. I take a bite of my salad and look around, spotting Kevin's two friends from his Instagram posts walking toward us. I sit up straight, trying to exude confidence I don't have.

"Hey, I am Tanya." The girl beams.

"And I am Tristan; nice to meet you," adds the boy, his ocean-blue eyes sparkling. I notice his tragus piercing and wince.

Tristan is very handsome and appears sure of himself, while Tanya seems like a "princess," judging by how prim and proper she is. Her eyes are light brown with a grayish tinge, and she wears a nose ring. She is beautiful.

"These are my only friends in this school; they are on the West Side, though. But I don't hold that against them." Kevin smirks.

They all laugh. Honestly, I don't see the joke, but it probably isn't meant for me to get.

"I thought the West and East Side don't interact with one another." I cross my arms and tilt my head as I look at them.

"Mostly, we don't. But we three hit it off so well in gym class we became friends," Tristan explained.

"Yeah, we have been cool ever since our first encounter." Kevin fist-pumps Tristan.

"So, how do you two know each other?" I look from Tristan to Tanya.

"We met on our seventeenth birthday." She stares intently at Tristan, and they share a long, sloppy kiss.

Well, I didn't see that coming.

"Great, those annoying twins have found me." Tanya scowls when she and Tristan break away from their kiss.

I am about to ask which twins she is talking about when I notice

Marissa and Crissy walking toward us.

"I thought norms are not supposed to sit with us?" Marissa grits her teeth.

"I'm sorry, and who are you? You're new here and should tread lightly with what you say!" Tanya retorts, causing a sadistic smirk to appear on Kevin's handsome face.

I feel like I belong for the first time in a long time. Finally, Marissa and her sister are on the other side, but I have to interject because of who I am.

"How about we all sit here and enjoy lunch together?" I suggest.

Marissa and Crissy scowl at me, and the next thing I know, I feel a smack across my face. *I'm sorry. Did she just slap me? I think she did!*

I stand up, clenching my fists. *Crissy smacked me across the face.* Everyone is now standing, and Kevin looks angry.

"I'm reporting you to the principal!" Tanya storms away, with Tristan following her.

What is happening? People are actually sticking up for me.

"Let's go!" Kevin grabs my hand to walk away, and I can't fathom what's happening. Besides my two best friends, no one has ever stuck up to a bully for me before. And even though I want to punch Crissy right in her big mouth, I let it go.

Once school is over, Kevin offers to drive me home, and he is adamant about telling my dad what happened at lunch today, which is amazing of him because until now, it has been as if the twins are angels when they are really Satan's spawns. Every time I tell my dad some evil thing they've done, Gabriella convinces him it was all a misunderstanding. So, I finally gave up trying.

I arrive home right before the demon twins and inform my dad about what happened with them in school and how Crissy smacked me in the face when I didn't even do anything. He is livid but thanks Kevin for stepping in and invites him to stay for dinner.

SEVENTEEN

Instead of the usual "family dinner" with the twins and Gabriella, there is a division for that night. Gabriella, Marissa, and Crissy go out while my dad, Kevin, and I stay in. If I am candid, this is for the best because my father, Kevin, and I get to spend quality time together. We have a great evening, and I look forward to more days like this.

Chapter 5

New Guy in School

IT HAS BEEN several weeks since Crissy smacked me in the face, and my father and Gabriella have not spoken during all this time. As a result, she sleeps in the guest room, and he sleeps in their bedroom. *If only they would get divorced!* I am grateful to Kevin, Tanya, and Tristan for sticking up for me because Gabriella cannot sweet-talk my dad into accepting her daughter's actions toward me this time. But, of course, it does not last long because soon she is prancing around the house in skimpy clothing and back in the room with my father. *It was good while it lasted.*

Usually, when the twins pick on me—mostly Marissa—Gabriella gives some ridiculous excuse for why they did it. But because Tanya defended me and reported them to the principal, her ploy didn't work this time, and my dad was over it. Still, I do not know what he sees in her.

Kevin is picking me up to go to school, which my father is a little skeptical about at first, but after a few dinner nights, he has become very fond of Kevin. Not to mention so am I, but I do not know what we are. We are more than friends, but neither of us has said if we are boyfriend and girlfriend, although it feels like we are.

We text each other every night, or he calls me. So, I feel like I am his girlfriend, but until he says so, I won't think more of it.

Kevin calls to let me know he is outside, and I see the twins give me a death glare as I walk out the door. Since the altercation, Tanya, *the most popular girl in school*, has given the twins a hard time. I can't believe she stuck up for me and has become such a lovely friend. But I do not believe in bullying, and when I voiced my concerns to Tanya, she understood. She still gives the twins the cold shoulder but does not bully them.

"Hey, babe," Kevin smoothly says as I climb into his 2021 Red Mustang Coupe.

"Hi." I giggle and kiss him on the cheek.

It has only been a few weeks, but I am smitten. Since that day at lunch, we have spent every day together. He even liked some of my posts on Instagram, but nothing is official yet. Once we arrive at school, we kiss and head to our classes.

I am in math class when the principal enters with a new guy. And *wow!* I think Kevin is hot, but I can't help but stare when I see this guy. We make eye contact but do not speak. There is something about him that is alluring. We have several classes together that day, and by our fifth one, I decide to introduce myself, but before I get the chance to do that, he taps me on my shoulder.

"Hi, my name is Eli Powers," he says, beating me to the punch and introducing himself first. "I've noticed that we're in a few classes together. What's your name?" His voice is deep and sensual, and the words flow from his lips like melted butter.

"My name is Claudette Richardson." I smile. "Nice to meet you."

"Nice to meet you, too." And as soon as he touches my hand, I feel electric shocks vibrating up my arm and releasing through my fingers. My heart sinks into my stomach, and I gasp for air. *What was that?* His intense gaze falls on mine, and we do not speak. He looks at his hand, and his lips curve into a smirk. I know he felt the electric shock as well.

He sits beside me, and I cannot help but check him out. He is tall, and his skin is like dark chocolate that could melt in your mouth. His eyes are light brown, and he wears his hair in a short fade haircut. He is fine. But I am taken, or at least I think I am.

"So, how old are you?" He leans in as he waits for my response.

My heart is pounding at the sound of his voice. It is like his words are vibrating throughout my body. "I'm sixteen. How old are you?" I finally say.

"I'm sixteen too, turning seventeen in a few weeks."

"Oh, when is your birthday?" The mention of his seventeenth birthday approaching in a few weeks piques my interest.

"March seventeenth. When's yours?" he asks. It's like we are playing a game of twenty-one questions.

"Oh wow! My birthday is March twentieth." My eyes sparkle.

His lips upturn into a smirk. "Do you have any plans?"

"Not at the moment, but can I ask you something?" I lean closer to him and lower my voice. "What is with this town and the big deal of turning seventeen?"

His eyes widen, and for a moment, I think he will not respond.

"Once my birthday comes around, I can tell you the significance since it seems to be such a huge thing in this town. Unfortunately, I won't know what the hype is about until then." He shakes his head.

"I look forward to that." I give him a satisfied smile.

He winks and starts collecting his books right before the bell rings. It is now time for lunch.

While walking to lunch, I notice a familiar face. *Isabel.* I have not seen Isabel since the day she tried to take her life. When I get a closer look at her, she seems different, but in a good way.

"Hi, Claudette!" she exclaims, skipping toward me.

"Hey Isabel, how are you?" I ask cautiously.

"I am great!" Her mood is the opposite of our last encounter. "I wanted to say thank you so much for saving my life last month. I was so broken."

I give her a small smile. "Don't mention it. I'm happy you're okay. Where have you been since?"

"I needed time to reflect on what had happened and make my decision."

My mouth forms a small O.

"Yeah, I'll catch you later, okay? We should hang out one of these days," she says, walking away toward the West Wing. *I wonder what decision she had to make.*

I'm in the cafeteria waiting in line to get my food when Eli's handsome self appears.

"Hey Claudette, want to sit together?" he asks.

I am flattered. "Hey, Eli. I'm sitting with my friends outside in the courtyard." I point to them.

"*Those* are your friends?" His eyebrows shoot up.

"Yes, they are. Why?" Before he can answer, Kevin is behind me, snaking his arm around my waist. Eli looks unamused.

"Who is this, babe?" Kevin asks, emphasizing the word "babe."

"This is my friend Eli. Eli, this is Kevin."

"Claudette's *boyfriend*," he interjects.

Um, what? Boyfriend?

"I didn't realize you had a boyfriend, Claudette," Eli says.

I didn't realize it, either.

"Would it be okay if Eli joined us for lunch?"

Kevin gives me a look, which is enough of a response.

"It's fine; I have something to do anyway," Eli states as he scurries away from us.

Kevin places his arm around my neck, and we head outside to the courtyard. Still confused, I stop before we reach Tanya and Tristan.

"What's wrong with you?" Kevin asks.

"Um... *boyfriend*?" I look at him expectantly.

"You're my girl," he says, leaning in closer, so his lips are only inches away from mine.

"There hasn't been any discussion of titles yet, so how was I to know I'm your girlfriend?" I give him a pointed look, but on the inside, I'm swooning at the words "my girl."

He pulls me into his arms and whispers, "You have been mine since the first day you arrived here."

Shivers run down my spine, and butterflies flutter in my gut. Kevin lifts my chin and presses his lips firmly against mine. The passion I feel behind the kiss is mind-blowing. He is teasing me and making me want more, and he knows it. I feel tingling throughout my entire body; I want him badly! But I think it's best to wait a little longer before moving to the next base. He clutches my breast with his right hand and growls quietly into my ear. My mind fills with nothing but dirty thoughts. For a moment, we forgot where we were—*in school!*

"What are you doing Friday night?" he asks, pulling me from my daydream.

"I don't have any plans," I say breathlessly.

"Now you do. I am taking you out, and I've already talked it over with your dad." He smiles slyly.

My eyes widen. "You did?" A massive grin forms on my lips.

"Of course, I already know I have to be on good terms with your dad." Kevin grins.

"Interesting. Where are you taking me?" I cock my head and regard him through narrowed eyes.

"It's a surprise, babe." He taps the tip of my nose. "Be ready at six p.m."

I nod, and then we join Tanya and Tristan at the table. Hanging out with them has become a ritual I enjoy a lot. They are fun and always keep me on my toes. Tanya and Tristan are like the perfect couple; it's as if they are fated to be together—if that is a thing. *I wonder if Kevin is my mate.*

The rest of the day breezes by, and Eli does not say much to me since Kevin dropped the "girlfriend" bombshell at lunch. After the bell rings for my last class, I am at my locker, stuffing my bag with books, when I notice Eli walking past me. I catch up with him. "Hey Eli, how was your first day of school?"

"It's been okay so far." He avoids eye contact while we walk down the hallway in sync. "This school is pretty weird."

"I agree. Totally bizarre, especially the students on the west side," I reply. It is refreshing to know that someone feels the same about this school.

"But I was wondering if we could exchange numbers. I'm behind on schoolwork, and I thought... maybe... we could be science partners? Don't worry; I understand you have a boyfriend. I am not trying to overstep," he hurries to assure me.

I am taken aback by his request. Judging from how Kevin looked at Eli, I know he would not be okay with this. But I do not have a science partner yet, and besides Kevin, I don't really speak to anyone on the east side. It wouldn't hurt to make a friend. "I wasn't worried, and of course, we can."

We swap phones to exchange numbers.

"Awesome! I'll catch you later," he says, turning in the opposite direction.

"See you tomorrow, Eli." I wave before heading toward Kevin's car.

I cannot tell if Kevin is jealous or not, but when I get in the car, he gives me a look and rolls his eyes in Eli's direction.

"We're just friends." I kiss him on the cheek.

His lips curve into a sinister smirk, and he speeds off, cutting Eli off in the parking lot.

"*Kevin!*" I screech.

He does not say a word and continues driving. We sit silently for a few minutes when we arrive at my house.

"I'm sorry, babe, but I don't trust him. He gives me a bad vibe."

Does he not trust Eli, or is this jealousy? "I understand, but I don't get a bad vibe from him, and he is new here like I am. Can you try to be nice to him for me?" I plead.

He strokes his chin hair and purses his lips. "Hmm, I'll try."

I roll my eyes before getting out of the car, then walk to the driver's side, lean in, and press my lips against his.

"See you later, babe." He winks and drives off.

Walking down our driveway, I am smiling from ear to ear. I am happy for once, although my dad and Gabriella are on better terms. But because of the incident with Crissy, we no longer eat dinner as a *"family,"* for which I am incredibly thankful. I grab some takeout my father had ordered and head to my room.

After taking a shower, I eat and begin scrolling on Instagram. When I notice a follow-request from Eli, I accept it and follow back. I am Kevin's "girlfriend," but there is nothing wrong with being friends with Eli, and besides, I do not get the bad vibe from him that Kevin claims he feels.

Chapter 6

Hot Date

TODAY IS FINALLY Friday, and I am getting dressed for my first hot date with the sexiest guy in my school. My father gave me "the talk" and told me not to do anything he would not do. This talk with him was highly uncomfortable, but I understood where he was coming from. Besides, I am not ready for sex, no matter how much my body says otherwise. Well, at least, *not yet*.

I stand in front of the mirror wearing a long, lavender, strapless dress that clings to my curves in all the right places. This dress means a lot to me because it was the dress my mom wore to her junior high school prom she attended with my father as her date. My father was very emotional when he pulled it out of storage. Although much time has passed since my mother died, I can still see the pain in his eyes. I wish she were here so we could gossip about boys, talk about girl stuff, and discuss the best panty to wear with my dress, but she was called to be an angel. I am trying my hardest to fight back the tears because I do not want to mess up the lovely makeup I spent so much time perfecting. I feel extremely uneasy, but I don't want the sadness to overturn my mood. Our first appointment is not for a couple of weeks, but I need to speak with my therapist. I still miss my mom every day. It's a sadness I will continue to carry, but thanks to Ms. Cameau's help, I've been learning to cope. I hope my new therapist can help me deal with the move, Gabriella, and her demon twins.

The doorbell rings. "Claudette, Kevin is here," my father announces. My heart drops, and butterflies flutter around in my stomach. I am incredibly nervous because I don't know what to expect. I have never been on a date before.

I head down the stairs and walk past the kitchen to the door to meet Kevin. Gabriella and the twins are in the living room, and I can see the hatred in their eyes. *If looks could kill, I would be dead.*

"Have a nice time," Gabriella says softly, a weird smile accompanying her words. Instead of replying, I merely give her a nod.

"Have a good time, sweetheart. Your curfew is at eleven p.m. Don't be late." My dad hands me the white shawl my mother wore with her dress, and I smile and embrace him.

Kevin's eyes widen when I place my hand in his as he helps me down the steps. He opens the car door and waits for me to get in like the handsome gentleman he is. He looks rather hot in his slim-fit black tux.

"Wow!" he exclaims.

"Wow, yourself!" I imitate. His lips curve into a wide grin. I don't know where we are going, but I am excited.

We drive a short distance before pulling into his apartment parking lot, and I am confused. I thought we were going to a restaurant or something. Not wanting to appear disappointed, I keep a poker face and wait for him to explain the meaning of us being at his apartment. *I hope he doesn't think I will lose my virginity to him tonight!*

"It's not what you think," he says, looking me in the eye, and I blush. "I made you dinner."

Umm. What?

"I wanted to make you a special dinner that reminded you of home, and then we will head back to your old town for dessert." He looks at me expectedly.

I can tell he is nervous, and it is so cute. "But I have to be home b–" I say before he cuts me off.

"I spoke to your father and informed him of our dinner plans. We're going to your favorite ice cream shop, Evi."

Did I hear him correctly? "We're going to Evi's?" My eyes sparkle.

"Yeah, babe." He smiles at my eagerness; it is the reaction he was hoping for. "I spoke to the shop owner and asked if she could keep the place open a little longer, and of course, once I presented her with money, she couldn't say no."

I thought I was at a loss for words when we were in the car, but when I walk into his apartment, I am overwhelmed with emotions; Kevin has outdone himself. Adorning the dining table is a white tablecloth, ivory napkins folded in a fancy design, and long-stemmed champagne flutes. Several covered platters are on the table, and a bottle of sparkling cider is chilling in an ice bucket at one end. Oh, and did I mention he has *china* plates? Like he brought out the fine dining plates for little old me!

Kevin pulls out a chair from the table for me to sit and hands me a napkin.

"What's on the menu for tonight?" I ask, my eyes shining. *Boy, am I hungry for Kevin's fine self, but I'll be a good girl and eat first.*

"I asked your father what your favorite meal was," he says in a low, sensual tone, uncovering the platters to reveal the yummy offerings. He has prepared a filet mignon cooked medium rare, with grilled asparagus and mashed potatoes for us. *Is he a chef? What seventeen-year-old can cook this well? I mean restaurant-quality*

51

food! It was as if Chef Gordon Ramsey had prepared the food for me. I am stunned.

Kevin sits across from me and says a quick prayer, and then we enjoy the fabulous meal he'd prepared. I am famished.

"How are you enjoying your steak?" he questions between bites.

I moan. "It's *delicious.*"

His eyes darken, and he clears his throat. "Uh, how was your day today?"

I can tell he's trying to distract his mind from the gutter and suppress a smile. "Okay, seriously, Kevin. What gives?"

"What do you mean?" He quirks his eyebrow.

"Where did you learn to cook like this?" I close my eyes and sink my teeth into the tender steak, enjoying its taste.

He shakes his head, laughing at me, and then his face grows serious. "It was self-taught. After my parents kicked me out, I had to learn how to fend for myself."

I stop chewing. "I didn't know that. Why did your parents kick you out?" My voice soothes.

"That's something to discuss in a few weeks when you turn seventeen."

I am so tired of this age discussion! I make a sour face and continue eating my delicious meal. Once we finish, Kevin places the dishes in the dishwasher, and we share the sweetest kiss. Every kiss with Kevin is better than the last. My knees are weak, and my body is ready to feel him inside me. However, I am determined to wait until the right time to give myself to him. *But if he keeps this up, it will be soon.*

"Claudette, I care for you," he declares after our lips part. The seriousness in his tone does not go unnoticed. His gaze is intense, and I feel his affection for me. *Is he the one?* He places two fingers beneath my chin and tilts my head until our eyes meet. My heart is racing as he leans in and presses his lips against mine again. His hands snake around my waist, pulling my frame closer to his, and I can feel a significant bulge pressing against my thighs.

"Are you ready to leave?" he says, his voice like a low growl, and I can tell he is trying hard to restrain himself.

"For what?" I shake my head slightly, trying to pull myself from the heat and sensation I feel down there.

"To head back to your old town for dessert?" He smirks.

"Oh yeah, that's right. I'm ready." I fumble with my words, and he grabs his keys from the holder where he'd placed them earlier.

My old town is about one hour away. When we finally arrive at Evi's ice cream shop, it is closed, but because Kevin gave her extra money, Evi is waiting and lets us inside. I order my favorite butter pecan ice cream, and Kevin gets strawberry, my mother's favorite. I feel goosebumps when he orders it. *Is this a sign?*

"What's on your mind?" he says when he notices me gaping at him.

"That... that ice cream. My mom." I cannot get the words out without being overwhelmed by emotions.

He grabs a napkin, folds it, and gently dabs at a tear rolling down my cheek. I clear my throat and speak again. "I'm sorry. My mom's favorite ice cream was strawberry."

"I apologize; I didn't know."

I can see the concern in his eyes.

"Don't be silly; how could you have known? I'm fine," I reassure him. "It just took me by surprise. You know I am wearing her dress tonight?"

"You look gorgeous, Claudette." He runs his eyes over my body, and I feel like he's touched me. He leans so close to me I can feel his breath on my lips. "I am glad I met you," he whispers.

I cannot help but smile; I am glad I met him, too.

We are enjoying our ice cream and chatting when suddenly Nicolette and Spencer enter the shop.

"*Oh, my gosh*! Did you invite them here?" I jump out of the booth and smother my friends with hugs, cheesing from ear to ear.

"Yes, he did! I like this one, Claudette." Nicolette grabs me in another bear hug.

"He is certainly a keeper," Spencer agrees.

"I missed you guys so much!" I am in awe. I cannot believe it. They are supposed to visit me for my birthday, but for some weird reason, they still cannot find my town on the GPS. I will have to give them the directions. I can't believe Kevin secretly contacted my friends and invited them to meet us! This is the best first date I have ever been on, and I will remember it for the rest of my life. Of course, this is the *only* date I have ever been on, so there is that. Even so, it is undoubtedly one for the books.

Grabbing Kevin by the collar, I kiss him passionately, licking him with my tongue and stroking his torso with my fingers, wanting him to feel how grateful I am.

"Woah, Claudette, you are in public! Calm that down!" Nicolette admonishes, holding out her hand.

"Let them enjoy themselves." Spencer grins as he watches us kissing.

I am in love with Kevin, or is this lust?

"Keep this up, and you will have all of me in no time," I whisper into Kevin's ear so that only he can hear.

He gives me a smirk. "I look forward to being inside you," he teases.

I want you inside of me now!

"Would you like to be my date for the early Spring Dance in a couple of weeks?"

I am smiling from ear to ear. "It would be my pleasure."

"The pleasure is all mine, beautiful," he says, giving me one of his sexy smiles.

We spend the next thirty minutes chatting about school and everything else we can think of. My two best friends are getting along with my boyfriend, and I adore it. After we leave the ice cream shop, we hold hands the entire way home. And when he drops me off, he gives me such a fiery kiss that I think I might combust.

"I want you to know how much you mean to me, Claudette," he says as our lips part. "I really care about you."

"I really care about you too, Kevin."

He gives me one last kiss before finally sending me inside. *This has indeed been the best date night ever!*

Chapter 7

Early Spring Dance

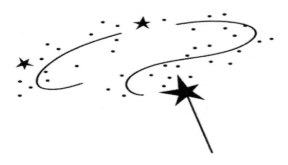

SEVERAL WEEKENDS LATER, and before you know it, it's Monday morning again, and I am heading to my first-period class. I spot Isabel on my way to class and approach her. "Hey Isabel, how are you?"

"Hi Claudette, I'm feeling good. Thank you for asking."

"I haven't seen you since the last time we spoke; are you sure everything's okay?" I tilt my head to one side as I look at her.

"Yes, I'm fine. I hate to sound like a broken record, but I will explain it to you in a few days." She smiles.

"Seventeen?" I screw up my face, and she just smiles and nods.

"I wanted to ask you something." She pauses, biting her lip. "Are you friends with Tanya, Tristan, and Kevin?"

Her question is unexpected, but I answer her. "Yes, and Kevin is kind of my boyfriend."

It seems weird saying it out loud, but oddly enough, I love how it sounds. But Isabel's expression says otherwise. I am about to say something about it when Kevin walks up and kisses the back of my neck.

"I'll catch you later," she says, scurrying away like Kevin has

57

stolen something from her.

I frown. "What was that about?"

Kevin shrugs. "I don't know. Isabel is super creepy."

"Is she now?" I purse my lips, staring after Isabel.

"Yeah, she is. Trust me, I've known her for years, and she is not right in the head." He twirls a finger beside one ear.

I nod, dismissing the subject, and we head to class.

The following five periods go by like a breeze. I am heading to the gym when I notice Eli, Isabel, another guy, and the same girl who had ushered Isabel from the bathroom on my first day, standing at a desk with sign-up sheets. *What is her name?* I intend to hurry past them, but Isabel and Eli flag me down. Eli is very handsome and welcoming, and I cannot help but feel drawn to him, but I already have an incredibly sexy boyfriend.

I stop and check out the sheet on the desk. It is a sign-up for the Early Spring Dance committee. I give them two thumbs up and walk away. I do not want to sign up for the dance committee, and who has a dance on a Tuesday, anyway? In my previous school, we always had our dances on Fridays.

"Hey Claudette, wait up," Eli calls after me. *Ugh. What does he want?* I turn to face him, my lips curving into a fake smile. *I have a boyfriend.* I repeat this mantra, trying to ignore my attraction to Eli.

"Hi Eli, how are you?" I ask through gritted teeth, swallowing a moan. *He is so sexy. Calm down, Detta!*

"I'm great." He flashes me his pearly whites. "I was wondering if you want to join the dance committee?"

"No," I reply without hesitation.

Eli laughs. I am unamused and look at him with a severe expression, which makes him laugh even harder.

"You know you're the first person to deny me like that?" He laughs so hard he is gasping for air.

I'm not surprised. I am more straightforward than most and don't want to plan the spring dance.

"Come on, Claudette, it will be fun, *and* tomorrow's my birthday," he coaxes.

Is that supposed to get me to change my mind? He grabs my hand, and I feel a jolt of electricity stream through my body, so intense I am shaken. And the way he sucks his bottom lip and glares at me lets me know he felt it too.

I jerk my hand away from his. "What was *that*?" I wrinkle my brow. It's the second time electricity has flowed between us.

"It means you should help with the dance." He smirks.

I really do not want to, but when he flashes me his dashing smile, I feel compelled to say yes. I reluctantly nod and follow him back to the table to sign up.

"We will meet here after school," Eli says.

"I can't. I have a meeting with my therapist." I bite my lip.

"Therapist? Is everything okay?" A look of concern fills his eyes.

"Yes... well, not really," I say. "I just have some things I need to sort out, and ah, that's what therapy is for, isn't it?" I swallow hard.

"I completely understand," Isabel chimes in. "I've been in therapy since my parents died."

I knew her parents had died from stalking her Instagram, but this was the first time I'd heard Isabel say it. "I am so sorry for your loss, Isabel."

"It's okay. I mean, it is what it is now. I am working through it." She shrugs.

The nameless girl from the bathroom rubs Isabel's back. "It will be okay, Izzy," she whispers.

"How about after you meet with your therapist, you meet us back here, so we can start planning? My father didn't leave much time for us to figure it out since the dance is tomorrow," the girl suggests. "I'm Destiny, by the way. The principal's daughter." She holds her hand to shake mine.

The handsome guy beside her shakes my hand and introduces himself, too. "I'm Lin; nice to meet you." His lips curve into a smile.

We go our separate ways, and I head to the girl's locker room to get ready for gym class. While I'm there, Destiny enters and gestures for me to meet her by the showers.

After I get dressed and place my belongings in the locker, I meet her by the broken shower. It's not actually broken, but we claim it is because it doesn't have hot water. It sucks when you don't get to the showers quickly enough, and it's the only one left.

"Hey Claudette, I wanted to thank you," Destiny says.

I scrunch up my face. "For...?"

"Stopping Isabel."

"Oh. I didn't really do anything. Are you and Isabel close?"

"Isabel is my girlfriend. She's been having a tough time since her parents' death. I have been trying to do everything that I can to keep her in a happy place. But it's hard to do that when people are being murdered left and right in this town."

Umm... I'm sorry; what does she mean by murdered "left and right?" I freeze, not knowing what to say, but I know she just said that. Like I heard her correctly–*didn't I?*

Not noticing my confusion, Destiny continues, "My mother was found dead three years ago, and now both of Isabel's parents are gone. I have been trying to figure out for weeks if one murder has anything to do with the other, but no luck."

I have no idea why she is telling me this or what I am supposed to do with the information, but I nod and try to keep my eyes from bugging out.

"My mom is gone too, but she wasn't murdered. She passed away from a heart attack when I was younger, so I understand losing a parent," I say. "I also understand wanting to commit suicide. There have been plenty of times when I just wanted the pain I felt to stop, and I tried to kill myself. Luckily, my father intervened. So, when I saw Isabel, I just wanted to help her, and I am glad she is doing better now."

"Oh no, I am so sorry you felt the need to want to do that." She rests her hand on my shoulder. "I can't imagine what you must have been thinking in those moments."

"All you feel is pain; that's what you're thinking about. You want the pain you feel to stop," I admit. "But people don't understand that the pain doesn't last, and better days are ahead. You just have to push forward to see them."

Destiny looks at me with complete understanding. "So many people don't see the bright light at the end of the tunnel. But thank you for helping my girlfriend when I couldn't be there. I can never thank you enough. I don't know what I would do if something ever happened to her." She wipes the tear that rolls down her cheek. "It's nice meeting you, Claudette, and I look forward to planning the dance with you later." She gives me a broad smile.

We embrace and head to the gym, where everyone sits, waiting for the activities to start.

After school, Kevin drops me off at my new therapist, Ms. Hudson's, office. It is actually her home, which I think is weird. But hey, to each his own.

Kevin kisses me and tells me he will return to pick me up after the session. I haven't told him I joined the school dance planning committee.

I enter the house through the unlocked door into a vast open area. Ms. Hudson's home is incredibly creepy, like something straight out of a haunted movie. Everything is black and gray; it's like she is unaware that an entire color palette exists with additional selections besides those two. In the waiting area are castle-like throne chairs engraved with full moons for her guests. I lower myself into one and wait for her to come out of her office to greet me.

"Hello dear, you must be Claudette," a gentle voice says.

I look up to see Ms. Hudson, a heavy-set, brown-haired woman with ocean-blue eyes, and stand to shake her hand. She wears bright red lipstick, a huge moon pendant necklace around her neck, and another dangling from a bracelet on her left arm. Aside from her creepy décor and appearance, her aura is extremely inviting.

"Let's go in here." She shows me into her office.

Along the walls are several photos of crescent moons. *What is this obsession she has with moons? Maybe she should speak to someone about this.*

She sits at a black and silver desk and reaches into the last drawer on the right side to pull out a black notebook. "Please take a seat." She points to a black two-seater sofa.

I sit and make myself comfortable, putting my bag on the floor and crossing my legs. The sofa is plush and comfy, and I want to fall asleep. I don't know what to say, so I wait for her to speak first.

She glances at me and writes in her little notebook.

I uncross my legs and shake my right leg vigorously, feeling my nerves build up.

"So, tell me about yourself?" she says finally, breaking the deafening silence.

I shift in my seat; I hate when people ask me about myself. I am not very interesting. "My name is Claudette," I state the obvious.

She gives me a soft smile and writes something down. "Yes, I know that. I would like you to tell me something new, or would you prefer I tell you about myself first?"

"How about you tell me about yourself?" *And this obsession with moons.*

"My name is Ms. Hudson. I am divorced and don't have any children. I have been a social worker for over twenty years and enjoy helping people. Now, would you like to tell me something about you?"

I gulp down the knot in my throat. "My mother died when I was younger, and my dad remarried to a woman I dislike. And I feel like she is the one that made us move here."

Ms. Hudson scribbles in her notebook quickly. "I see. First, I would like to say I am sorry for your loss. Second, how do you feel about living here?"

"Thank you." I give her a small smile. "I don't like this town much. I miss my home, but I met this awesome guy."

"Yes, Mr. Evans."

"Yes, you know him?" I watch her through narrowed eyes. *How does she know about Kevin and me?*

"This is a tiny town; I know everyone here." She chuckles.

"Oh, of course." I feel my face grow hot.

"Claudette, what do you want to gain from our sessions?" She studies me, waiting for my answer.

"Honestly, I need help dealing with this move. Sometimes, I get this overwhelming feeling that I am missing something, but I don't know or understand what. And I miss my mother; I really wish she were alive, especially at times like this, when I have a boyfriend. I wish she were here so I could have 'girl talk' with her. Before she died, we were so close. I know we would have become even closer had she lived. I envy the girls who still have their moms." The words came out of me like vomit; there it was, the one thing I could never say to Ms. Cameau. *I envy girls with mothers.*

We both knew that I was grieving for my mother, but I would

spend most of my time talking about other stuff or complaining about the twins. The fact of the matter was I miss my mother, and now that I have a boyfriend, I miss her even more.

As I speak, my feelings overwhelm me, and I begin to sob, deep sobs that wrack my entire body. Ms. Hudson stands up to hand me a box of Kleenex. By the time I am done, I'm sure I have used most of the box, but when I glance at her bookshelf, I see she has a large stack of Kleenex. *I guess she is used to this.* By the time the session ends, I feel comfortable with Ms. Hudson. The session went well, and I am thankful Ms. Cameau recommended her.

After my session, Kevin picks me up, and I ask him to drop me off at school. He is unhappy about me planning the school dance with Destiny, Eli, Lin, and Isabel. I do not know what bad blood is between them, but I intend to find out.

I walk down the hallway to the gym; we have about two hours to figure out what we want to do regarding plans for the dance. We sit in a circle, bouncing ideas off one another until we finally decide on a Halloween-themed dance. I do not know how we came up with the idea, but I am all for it.

Afterward, Destiny drops me at home, and I am ready to crash when my dad knocks on my door. "Come in."

"Hey, Cheetah, how was your session today?" Dad gently tucks my baby hair behind my ear.

"It was great; I really like her." I yawn.

"That's fantastic!" he says, clapping his hands together.

"Yeah, I like her… but Dad, I am exhausted and ready for bed. Tomorrow is the school dance, and I need my beauty sleep." I push him toward the door.

He turns to kiss me on the forehead, then leaves.

I dive headfirst into my bed, not even bothering to shower or brush my teeth; I am just too drained.

SEVENTEEN

The following morning, I wake refreshed; I brush my teeth, shower, and prepare for school. Because the dance is today, we only have classes until the fifth period; we have lunch at sixth and will spend the seventh period decorating the gym for the dance. I didn't know what I wanted to wear or even what I wanted to be until Eli mentioned he had an extra pair of vampire teeth that I could use. This is awesome because I can wear anything black to go with that.

I finish a few minor details on my uniform, put on some stud earrings, and head downstairs to wait for Kevin to pick me up. The best thing about Crissy smacking me in the face is since that day, Kevin vowed to pick me up and drop me off at school. I have my license but no car. And if something happens between Kevin and me, I know Destiny, Eli, or Isabel would not mind driving me to school.

As I walk to the door, Marissa and Crissy block my way with their arms folded and scowls plastered on their faces.

"Move!" I place my hands on my hips and glower at them.

When we were at our old school, where they ruled as Queen B's, I would not have dared to say that to them, but since they are not in charge at Mashal High, I feel bold. At that moment, confidence flows throughout my entire body. For years, the two have tormented me, making fun of my skin color and calling me names such as blacky, dark thunder, and shadow. Finally, they can no longer bully me and make me feel low about myself, and I know it is getting to them.

"Excuse me, who do you think you're talking to... *Dark Thunder*?" Marissa says through gritted teeth.

"I am speaking to someone who is not happy with their own life and is completely pathetic. Now, move! My *boyfriend*, which neither of you has, is waiting for me outside." Watching their mouths fall open, I give them a self-satisfied smile.

65

Crissy is about to smack me again, but I grab her hand. "Not this time." I use all my strength to crush her hand. Marissa pushes me, and I push her back. The next thing I know, we are fighting. My father is off work today, and he and Gabriella break us up.

"I am so sick of those demon twins! I don't understand why you had to marry that awful woman and bring them into our lives!" I screech before storming out of the house, slamming the door behind me.

Kevin approaches me quickly as I stomp down the walkway toward his car.

"What happened?" He glances at my house, then looks back at me warily.

"I don't want to talk about it!" I snap. He does not say a word after my outburst and instead opens the car door for me, and we drive off in silence.

When we arrive at school, I am still very heated over what happened and do not want to discuss it. I go to my classes, and by sixth period I am over it. My dad sends me several text messages throughout the day that I ignore. I do not see the twins for the day; from the looks of it, it does not seem like they will appear at the dance.

The bell rings, and it is time to decorate the gym. Destiny, Isabel, and Lin are already decorating when I arrive, but I don't see Eli. "Hey, where is Eli?"

"He's running late; he should be here shortly," Destiny replies.

"Did you guys get him a birthday cake?" I ask.

"We were, but then he told us he didn't want one," Isabel says.

"He isn't into those types of things," Lin adds.

We are blowing up red, black, and gold balloons and putting streamers up when Eli walks in. He does not look like himself; he seems... well, I do not know what he looks like, but it is troubling.

I place my hand gently on his arm. "Are you okay?"

"I'm fine! I just want this day to be over," he snaps.

"Wait, what?" His reaction catches me off guard.

"Don't worry about it." He waves me off.

"But—"

"Let's just get these decorations up," he hisses, cutting me off.

I cannot understand what is wrong with him, but it does not seem to faze Destiny or Isabel. They completely ignore Eli's mood, and Lin, too, acts as if nothing is happening. So, I do the same.

After we finish with the gym, I go to the girl's locker room to change my outfit. I return to find the DJ setting up his equipment and chaperones walking around as students enter. Kevin arrives, looking very handsome in gray slacks and a slim-fit, button-down black shirt.

"What are you supposed to be?" I ask, grabbing him by the waist.

"I see you're feeling better now." He smiles and kisses me on the cheek.

"Yes." I swallow, feeling my cheeks turn red. "I'm sorry for snapping at you earlier."

"Shh." He puts a finger to his lips. "Don't tell anyone, but I am a warlock." He grins, lightening the mood.

I twirl. "I am a vampire. You like?"

He waggles his eyebrows at me, then gestures to the dance floor. "Would you like to dance?"

I nod, and he leads the way.

When he places his hands on my waist and pulls me close, I can feel the entire frame of his body pressing against mine. While we dance, it's like we are the only two people in the room. It is magical until the lightbulbs shatter.

Chapter 8

Seventeenth Birthday

ALL THE LIGHTBULBS shatter, and the windows explode. The shattered glass levitates above us. Yeah, you read that right. *The glass is levitating.* Everyone is on the floor, screaming. Kevin shields me during the chaos and points toward a table where we can hide.

"Kevin, what is happening?" I shriek.

"I am not sure, but we must get out of here!"

"How do you suggest we do that?"

"Follow me." He crawls on the floor toward a tiny door, and I follow suit. I would not have noticed it if we were not crawling toward it. Once the glass pieces fall out of the air, everyone goes into panic mode, running for the exits. It's like a stampede of animals trying to avoid being eaten by a lion. A piece of glass slices down my arm just as Kevin yanks me through the small crawl space down a secret tunnel out of the gym. He takes my arm and checks the wound as soon as we're out. I pull away, pacing back and forth. I cannot believe what I just saw. *Did the glass levitate, or am I going crazy?*

"Kevin, I need you to explain to me *now*! What just happened? And do not tell me to wait until I am seventeen because I will be in just a few days!" I cross my arms, tapping my right foot repeatedly on the floor.

He does not respond. "Kevin, seriously?" I roll my eyes. "I will be seventeen on Friday." I tighten my jaw and glare at him.

Still not a word. *Can you believe this guy?* I shake my head and turn around, looking for a way out of whatever secret closet we're in. Finding a door behind a bunch of dusty clothes, I am about to open it when Kevin grasps my hand.

"Magic is real." His voice is so low that I'm not sure I heard him correctly. I stick my index finger into my ear, trying to clear it of whatever might be blocking my hearing. Perhaps I have some earwax I need to clean out. "I'm sorry... *what?*"

"Magic. Is. Real." He enunciates each word. He says nothing else for a long moment, and just when I'm about to freak out, he speaks again. "Listen, Claudette. Please stay calm! No one can know that I told you. I understand you will be seventeen in three days, but there are rules in this town that we cannot–*should not*–break. My telling you magic is real is against the rules. Eli has broken the rules, too." By now, Kevin is rambling.

"*What?*"

He places a finger to my lips, indicating I should be quiet.

"What do you mean Eli broke the rules?" I whisper.

Kevin takes a step back and exhales.

"This town is full of witches and warlocks. On your seventeenth birthday, you will receive the gift–or curse, depending on your perspective–of magic and must decide whether you want to accept it. If you do, you will become a witch. If not, you will remain human. Today is Eli's seventeenth birthday; he accepted the magic. All the chaos in the gym happened because of his choice," Kevin explains.

Have you ever watched a cartoon where something surprising

happens, and your mouth drops to the floor? Well, this is no cartoon, but my mouth hangs wide open. I cock my head and place one hand on my throat, opening and closing it as if trying to ease an itch while I try to figure out the right words to say. When I open my mouth to speak, no words come out. I mean, I am mute.

"When we leave this closet, I need you to promise me you will not say a word to anyone about what I've told you." Kevin's pleading eyes fix on mine.

I stare at him blankly, still mute.

"Claudette!" He grabs my shoulders and gives me a slight shake.

"Who would believe me, anyway? I'm not even sure I believe it," I say, finally.

Which is true; I do not know what to believe. But then again, I trust what I saw with my own eyes. Glass levitated in the air, and Eli had acted weirdly. Yeah, I hardly know the guy, but going from being extremely friendly to ice-cold is a complete turnaround.

Kevin opens the door, and I see we are outside the school in the back parking lot. I can hear police cars and the fire truck coming to the rescue.

Kevin examines my arm. "You don't need stitches." He takes my hand and speed walks to his car. Once inside the vehicle, I cannot help myself. I have questions and need answers—*now*.

"Kevin, can you please pull over?" He glances at me and pulls over at the next light, parking in a fast-food lot underneath a tree.

"Did you want to make out?" he teases, trying to lighten the mood. His lips curve into a smirk when I roll my eyes.

He sighs. "Ask away, Claudette."

"What do you mean, magic is real? You said there are witches and warlocks in this town? Are you a warlock? Explain everything to me, Kevin, and please be honest."

"This town is full of witches and warlocks—" he begins, but I cut him off.

"Kevin!"

"Listen, Claudette. I will explain everything. But let me do it my way. Okay?" he scolds, and I keep my mouth shut.

"As I was saying before you so rudely interrupted." He tosses me a smile. "This town is full of witches and warlocks. There are Sun, Moon, and Earth witches. When you turn seventeen, you can keep your magic and develop it or get rid of it. When I turned seventeen, I opted to get rid of it; I felt like it was a curse. When you reach your seventeenth birthday on Friday, you will wake up not feeling like yourself. Some witches wake up angry; others are extremely sad. There is no in-between. The day you met Isabel was her seventeenth birthday, and she was tremendously sad but then decided to keep her magic, which is why she now has her classes in the West Wing. The West Wing students are 'Mags' because they practice magic, and the East Wing students are 'Norms.' We are the ones who decided we'd rather be normal than deal with the burden of possessing magic. My family are Sun witches, Eli is a Moon witch, Tristan and Tanya are Sun witches, and you, my beautiful girlfriend, are an Earth witch, which is very rare. The prophecy says I would fall in love with an Earth witch. It is why we have such a strong connection. I have felt drawn to you ever since we met. There is no doubt in my mind that we are meant to be together. As for your magic, I respect whatever decision you make. The look on your face tells me you are having difficulty believing what I'm telling you. But I want you to pay attention tomorrow. You will notice Eli is no longer in your classes; he may not even be in school. Isabel missed several days when she accepted her magic." Kevin's speech is very rapid now. I absorb every sentence, clinging to his every word.

"Are my stepsister's witches?" I ask.

"They accepted magic."

"Why haven't they tried to hurt me using their powers?"

"The rules forbid witches from using magic against norms. If they do, their power could be taken from them," he explains.

"Who would take their magic?"

"The Witch Council would conduct a ceremony using a dagger called a 'Ce-Ja' and recite a spell that takes away the power. There is a way to get the magic back, but that would require death and a lot of dark magic."

"Is my father a witch?" I cannot contain all my questions. The more Kevin tells me, the more I want to know; my curiosity increases, just like my nervousness.

"Your father rejected magic, as did your mother. That's why they could move out of town. But when two norms leave the town, they must return if they have a child, so the child can decide to remain normal or become a mag."

That made little sense to me; why go through all that trouble to move just to come back? "Does Gabriella practice magic?"

"No, she doesn't. The Witch Council took her magic away when she returned. Your father, Gabriella, and the twins had no choice but to move back to this town so that you could decide if you wanted to remain a norm or become a mag." Kevin looks me in the eye.

"I don't understand. The twins have been seventeen for two months now. Why didn't we move here before their seventeenth birthday? Or why did they leave in the first place?" I ask. There is so much I need to know, and I realize Kevin does not have all the answers.

"Honestly, I don't know. Gabriella accepted magic, so she should have never left this town," he says. "Claudette, I am sorry to tell you, but Gabriella and the twins leaving was against the rules. The twins still have their magic because they didn't have a say in leaving. But as soon as you arrived, the council summoned Gabriella and removed her magic. If you are a mag, you must stay in this town, no matter what. After the father of her children left without a word, Gabriella decided she would leave, according to what my mother said. And for years, the council searched for her; it wasn't until she married your father that she appeared on the radar again."

I honestly cannot fathom all this information. How can I go home and pretend I know nothing? *Wait? How can I go home?* With all this witch information and chaos at the dance, I completely forgot what transpired before I left home today. I am not going back to that house! I need time to digest everything about the rules, witches, and magic.

"Can I stay with you for the rest of the week?" I whisper. "I need time to process everything, and I would rather be around someone I can trust."

Kevin nods, starts the car, and we drive to his apartment. I am mentally and physically drained.

When we arrive at his apartment, I check my phone and see five missed calls from my dad. I do not want to speak to him. He is a liar. I should have known I was born a witch and would be burdened with this decision to remain a norm or become a mag. My eyes fill with tears as I think about all the times he could have told me. I do not need to wait until Friday to know I do not want to be a witch. I do not want to possess magic so powerful that I have glass levitating. *That is insane.*

"Babe, are you okay?" Kevin asks, breaking my train of thought.

"No, I am not okay," I confess. "My father has been lying to me my entire life. He could have told me before that I was a witch."

Kevin nods his head understandingly and embraces me. "Babe,

they moved to the real world. They could have told you that you were a witch. But then again, would you have been able to keep that to yourself? I mean, what child can keep that a secret from their friends? Which reminds me, you can't tell Nicolette or Spencer that you are a witch." He gazes into my eyes. "I mean it."

"I won't say anything to them," I lie. Of course, I will tell my two best friends, but I doubt they will believe me, anyway. Kevin gives me one of his black t-shirts and a brand-new toothbrush, and I head to the bathroom and shower. Afterward, I shoot my father a text.

Me: I need time to think. I am staying with Kevin for the rest of the week.

I don't wait for a response, and I'm not in the mood to eat, so I head straight to bed. Kevin, the gentleman he is, sleeps on the sofa in the living room.

The following day, I get dressed, still completely drained. It is Wednesday, and I am counting the hours until my birthday. Usually, I would be excited, but I dread the moment the magic that will soon awaken inside me. I stride toward the kitchen, where Kevin is in his boxers, cooking breakfast. *I could get used to this.* He greets me with a soft kiss and hands me a plate ladened with eggs, a biscuit, and French toast.

"You didn't eat last night, so I made you breakfast," he says. "What would you like to do for your birthday?" He wraps his arms around my waist.

"Hide in a storage facility," I blurt out.

He bursts out laughing. I am not sure what is so funny because I am completely serious.

"No, seriously, Claudette." He looms over me and looks at me with seriousness.

"Kevin, we don't know if I will be happy or sad that day. What makes you think I want to do something, especially after what happened with Eli?"

"Did you decide if you want to be a witch?" he asks.

I look at him with confidence. "Yes, I have already made my decision."

Kevin nods. "Tanya told me that when you decide before your birthday, sometimes you are sad; when you are conflicted about what you should do, you wake up angry. She is a part of the Witch Council tasked with monitoring the reactions. And so is Tristan."

"I don't want to be sad." Flashes of Isabel standing outside the window about to jump appear.

"Don't worry, I will be with you," he consoles.

"How long does it take for your magic to disappear?" I ask, pursing my lips.

"Whether you decide to become a mag or remain a norm, you will possess magic for seventeen days. Your magic will progress if you become a mag. If you decide to remain a norm, the magic will digress. If you are conflicted, then during that time, you will become angry."

A sudden thought comes to me. "Can you become evil?" I look up at him.

"Just don't let the magic consume you."

What does that even mean? "How do I prevent that from happening?"

"Let's finish getting ready for school. And please pretend you don't know any of this information," he pleads again, and I nod.

I scarf down the rest of my breakfast while Kevin gets ready for school.

When we arrive, I realize I am literally the only student in school who is unaware of magic. Also, no one discusses what happened at the dance, and all my friends avoid me throughout the day.

Isabel, Destiny, Lin, and Eli are missing in action, and when I go to lunch, Tanya and Tristan are nowhere to be found. To keep up the pretense, I go to the office and ask Principal Deanwall what happened in the gym yesterday. He tells me it was some electrical wiring and not to worry about it. It amazes me how everyone is in one accord to keep me in the dark.

After school, I listen to all my voicemails from Dad. He goes from angry to worried and back to angry. I send him a text.

Me: I need time.

Dad: Is it the twins?

I know I was not supposed to say anything, but unlike my father, I am not a liar.

Me: No. I hate the demon twins, but I'm used to their behavior. But you, Dad. I trusted you, and you lied to me. For years!

After I send him the text, I am having second thoughts. I wasn't supposed to know any of this, and now I have revealed it to my dad.

Dad: You know?

Me: What do you think?

I respond without second guessing it.

Dad: Please come home, so we can discuss this in person... or at least let me know your decision.

Me: Why should I?

Dad: Claudette, please. I know I have much to explain, but whatever you decide, I will support you.

After I don't respond, he calls me. Presumably, to ensure nothing gets lost in translation. I speak to him for about twenty minutes and tell him I do not want him to choose between his wife and me, so I decided for him. I will not live at home as long as Gabriella and the demon twins are there.

I give Kevin my keys to the house and ask him to pick up my

possessions because I cannot bear to look at my dad's face. When Kevin gets back with my belongings, he seems upset. He knows I revealed to my father that I have learned about witches, but I tell him I could not keep it from my father. I know my dad will say nothing to the council or Gabriella. As far as Gabriella and the others are concerned, my reason for not returning home is the fight I had with the twins. I told Dad to tell his wife I did not feel safe around the twins because they could jump me.

After Kevin and I eat dinner, we head to bed, and I set the timer on my watch until my birthday. This time, I curl up next to Kevin and fall asleep. He is so sexy, but I can't think about that now. But I know it will be perfect when I finally give myself to him.

Sixteen hours until my birthday...

When I awake the following morning, I feel exceedingly anxious. It is mere hours before I am seventeen years old. My friends send me text messages asking what I want to do for my birthday, but I ignore them. I do not know what to tell them.

Eli is a no-show again when we arrive at school, and so are Isabel, Destiny, Lin, Marissa, and Crissy. It's as if they purposely missed school so they would not risk me possibly asking questions. I feel like a robot attending all my classes. I am there physically but not mentally. Luckily, the day goes by quickly, and I am back at Kevin's apartment. Kevin is not at home; he told me he had to meet Tanya and Tristan and would be home later before my birthday to help me through it. I shower and wash my hair, which calms my nerves enough to eat dinner without vomiting. I look at the clock, and it is almost six pm.

SIX HOURS TO GO...

Sitting in the chair, rocking back and forth, I am petrified. I turn on the TV and flip through the channels, trying to find something to watch to take my mind off my impending doom. But nothing calms me.

When Kevin returns, he has a worried expression. I look at the time; it is almost eleven pm. He embraces me, and we watch the clock until it is midnight.

The lights begin to flicker off and on, and I feel a jolt of electricity flow through me like I am being electrocuted. I scream as I start to levitate. I have no control over what is happening. My entire body is shaking uncontrollably. I try to reach down to Kevin, but there is nothing he or I can do to stop what is happening to me.

Blue, gold, and black lights glisten along my arms and legs and finally emerge from my hands. I feel the magic awakening from deep within as my body finally descends. The room goes dark for about five minutes, and then the lights flicker on from a mere thought. *Did I do that?* When I point to a dish on the table, it falls to the floor, shattering. I cannot believe what is happening. *I have magical powers.*

Chapter 9

What Should I Do?

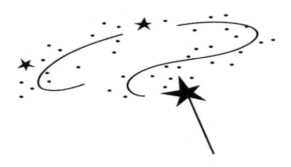

THE NEXT MORNING, I don't attend school. No one is surprised, however, because they all know it's my birthday. Kevin and I barely slept the night before; my magic seems to progress by the hour. It is as simple as thinking about what I want, and it happens. As soon as I think about butter pecan ice cream, it appears. It's my favorite flavor from Evi's ice cream shop. I sit on the sofa, trying to understand the magic growing inside me, and I can't fathom it. I never thought witches were real, let alone that I would be one.

To take my mind off what is happening, I decide to watch TV, but I can't find the remote. As soon as I think about it, it appears in my hand. *Woah!* Suddenly, I feel a rage building up inside of me. *No! I don't want to be a witch! Are you sure?* Detta, my inner voice entices me. Kevin explained that if I feel rage, it is because mentally, I want to become a mag. Even though I had decided to reject magic, I found it difficult to resist.

Kevin is in the shower, and I can feel myself getting angrier. I stand, throw the remote to the floor, storm into Kevin's room, and get dressed. The lights flicker on and off as I clench my fists. *Why is this happening?* The lights flickering upsets me even more.

"*Enough!*" I shout. The lights stop flashing, and the window explodes. Shards of glass fly around, and a piece slices my face.

Kevin rushes out of the bathroom, looking panicked, and sees the blood trickling down my face. "You're accepting the magic!" he exclaims.

"*What? No, I am not!* I don't want this." *Yes, you do!* I plummet to the floor, covering the cut on my face with one hand. "I don't want this!" I sob, grabbing Kevin by the leg. "Please make this stop!" *I don't want this magic; I don't want to be a mag. I want to be normal.*

The lights flicker again, and the bed levitates. Then everything in the room swirls around like a tornado. Chaos surrounds me, and I can't stop it. *I need to get out of here!*

I want my shoes, and they appear on my feet. Kevin is confused and asks where I am going, but I ignore him. There is only one person I want to see who will understand what I am going through right now. That's who I need to speak with—*Eli!*

When I open the front door, Eli is standing there. I get into the car with him, and we drive to his place in silence. When we arrive, neither of us speaks. I just want to get inside. I sit on the floor in a corner facing the wall as everything in his apartment shakes.

"Claudette?" he says.

Rage bursts from my body. "*What?!*"

"I need you to calm down. You can control the magic; don't let it control you. Just breathe and accept it."

"No, I don't want to accept it. I don't want to be a witch. Is that what you did? You accepted *this*?" My voice breaks, and I sob, shaking uncontrollably. I don't want to be a witch. "Please, please, Eli... help me."

He walks toward me slowly, holding his hands up as though confirming he is no threat. He reaches for my hand and helps me to my feet. My breaths slow as I calm down, and all the chaos in the room subsides. It is like someone watching this unfold hit the pause button on a remote; it is astounding.

"Did you do this?" I question.

"Yes, I used my magic to keep you calm and stopped all this." He makes a sweeping gesture around the room. "Here, drink this to calm your nerves." He hands me a cup of red juice.

I gulp it down in one sitting. "How did you do that?" I wipe my mouth with my sleeve.

"Control."

Something has changed with Eli. He is sure of himself and his magic. I don't know if I could be as confident as he is.

"Your body is reacting this way because you are telling yourself that you don't want to be a mag, but it's your fate to be one. Everything you did today before you lost control, deep down, you enjoyed it." He smiles.

I mean, when my favorite ice cream appeared in my hands, I did like it. Magic is tempting. I can't deny that.

He takes my hand and places it over the cut on my face. "Heal yourself."

My eyes widen at the thought that I can actually heal myself.

He nods, assuring me I can do it.

I close my eyes, take a deep breath, and my cut disappears. "Eli! The cut... it's gone; the pain is gone!" My eyes sparkle, and I feel in control. I wave my hand and return all the items in the room to their rightful places.

Eli's lips curve into a warm smile, and he embraces me. As soon as he touches me, I feel a shudder of energy. I can feel our magic entwining. The electricity streams through my body and into his. Blue, gold, and brown lights encircle our fingers, and it is as if we are complete. I feel drawn to him; *I want him!*

Eli caresses my lips with his thumb. When our gazes lock, he pulls me in for a soft kiss. While he teases me, circling his tongue in my mouth, I inhale his natural musk and close my eyes. When our lips part, we stare at each other. I felt the attraction between us the day we first met, but my feelings now are different. Our magic is connected, and I feel complete and lost in its union. So much so that I totally forgot... *I have a boyfriend!*

"What's wrong?" Eli strokes my cheek.

"Eli, we can't do this. I have a boyfriend." I push him back so we have some space between us.

"Do you really think Kevin is trustworthy?" His eyes darken.

"What do you mean?" I frown.

"What has Kevin told you about all this witch stuff?"

Before I can respond, he places his index finger over my lips, preventing me from speaking. "Let me tell you a story."

I slowly nod for him to proceed.

"Kevin's parents are both powerful Sun witches. Two witches of the same power uniting were unheard of until their union. It has always been Sun and Moon or Sun and Earth. In History of Magic, taught by Mr. Goatfair, two witches with the same power should not marry—Sun with Sun, Moon with Moon, Earth with Earth. When two witches with the same power bond and have a baby, that child is evil. While we all can use our magic for good or evil, you don't get to choose when born from the same coven. Kevin is not who he says he is. He didn't give up his powers. The council took his powers because he was evil. He doesn't live with his parents because they kicked him out. After that, my mom removed his parents from the witch's council. Rumors say he has been murdering the few Earth witches left in this town to regain his magic."

I can't grasp what Eli is telling me. Kevin isn't evil... he can't be. He loves me! There is no way Kevin could have been deceiving me this entire time. Kevin said he didn't want to be a mag and chose to remain a norm. If what Eli says is true, wouldn't Kevin be in jail? Or worse?

"You're just saying that!" I glare at Eli.

"Why would I make something like this up? I am sure he told you a nice little story about wanting to be a norm, but that's not true."

"How would you even know any of this? Aren't you new to this school?" Why is Eli telling me this? Kevin has been an incredible boyfriend, and I believe he cares for me. Which makes me feel even worse about the kiss Eli and I shared. The connection I feel with Eli is unimaginable, but no! This has to be a lie! *I'm an awful girlfriend!*

"Claudette! You don't attend Mashal High until you are sixteen years old. Before then, you go to a different school. I have lived in this town my entire life, and my parents are on the Witch Council."

My eyes widen at the mention of the Witch Council once again. Kevin said that Tanya and Tristan were on the council.

"Tristan and Tanya are Sun witches, and they are together. Why is that if it is forbidden?" I cross my arms and stare at Eli, waiting for an answer.

"You can't trust Kevin, Tristan, and Tanya. They are all evil, and they are planning something. Has Kevin suggested that you stay a norm or become a mag?"

I couldn't believe this; Tanya has been nothing but supportive. Tristan is funny, and Kevin is my boyfriend. I love him. But why would Eli say this? Why would he make this up? *He's jealous!*

"He told me he supported whatever decision I made. And I have decided that I want to be a witch." I stagger to the sofa and sit down. Eli has told me a lot, and I need time to process it. I cover my face with my hands, closing my eyes. *What should I do?* Kevin doesn't seem evil; he has been incredible since I met him. But there is this connection between Eli and me that I can't deny. Whenever we touch, electric shocks overwhelm me. It was as if our magic was trying to connect, and tonight, it finally did.

"I am telling you the truth." Eli ran his hands through his hair.

I take a deep breath, not looking at him. I need to ask Kevin myself. Did he lose his magic, or did he give it up as he said? I stand. I am going to find out.

"Where are you going?"

"I am going to ask my boyfriend myself!" I shout.

"You can't be serious! Claudette, he is using you!" Eli grabs me by the arm, preventing me from opening the door.

"Eli! Let go of me. I am going to ask Kevin myself. *Now let go!*" I feel my powers coming to the surface, and Eli goes flying. Rolling my eyes, I open the door to leave. I can't believe he thought he could prevent me from leaving.

Hmm... If I think about Kevin's place, will I appear there? As my thought ends, I materialize in front of Kevin's apartment, and I look around, wondering if anyone else has seen me pop up out of nowhere. But even if they did, so what? This is a town full of witches.

I knock and wait for Kevin to open it. He seems relieved when he opens the door, and our gazes meet. He leans in to embrace me. Although I feel conflicted, he came to the door with no shirt on, showing his massive abs and low-cut pants, and everything I am feeling goes away—*briefly*.

"We need to talk." I move to push past him, and he backs up with both hands in the air.

"*Are both your parents Sun witches?*" I demand so loudly I am sure the neighbors can hear me.

"Is that what Eli told you?"

"Umm... you don't answer a question with a question." I roll my eyes.

"Yes, my parents are both Sun witches."

I turn to leave, but he runs before me, holding his hands out to make me stop. "But please, babe, let me explain."

I tap my watch and give him the death glare. "Do not lie to me, Kevin," I say through gritted teeth. "You're walking on very thin ice."

"Okay, my parents fell in love with one another despite the rule, and when they were told that I would be evil, they took my magic away so that I would never have the burden of having to choose. I didn't make the choice. They made it for me."

So, he lied to me? What else has he lied about? "Is it true that you have murdered Earth witches to regain your magic?"

"What? No! I don't want magic and would never hurt anyone to get it. Claudette, do you really think I could murder someone?" He steps closer to me. I stare at him, not knowing whether to believe him. His eyes are clear, and he seems sincere.

"Claudette, I love you, and I know you can sense how you make me feel." He moves closer, and I notice a bulge in his pants. *Are you sure it's not just lust?* I step away from him and pace back and forth. Eli said they took away his magic because he was evil; now Kevin is telling me they took it away, but that didn't mean he was bad. I don't know what to believe.

"From what Eli told me, you don't have the choice in whether you are good or evil. You are just evil."

"I don't believe in all the old stories I've heard. I am my own person, and I choose to be good. Besides, evil cannot love, and I know I love you." Walking toward me, he leans in and kisses me on the cheek. My senses are on high alert, and I want him, but I don't feel the jolt of electricity I felt when Eli kissed me.

"Let me show you how you make me feel." He picks me up and

takes me into his bedroom. Sitting me on the bed, he takes off my shoes. I am about to say something when he kisses me, using his tongue this time, teasing me with it. I lose my train of thought. I am unsure if I am ready for what will happen next. My heart is racing so fast I think it will come out of my chest and land on the floor. He unbuttons my skinny jeans, looking me in the eye as he pulls them off. The anticipation of what he will do next sends my hormones into overdrive. He licks my inner thighs, still holding my eyes with his intense gaze. Working his way up my torso, he slightly lifts my shirt to reveal my purple sports bra, kissing me as he does so. Then he pulls my shirt over my head. My body feels like jelly, yet I am stiff. I let him do what he wants to me. Eyes still locked on mine, he gets off the bed and pulls down his pants, exposing his length. I can't take my eyes off him. I am ready for what is about to happen.

After lying on the bed, he kisses and licks my neck and slides his right hand inside my underwear. I moan as he pleasures me. He stops and stares at me, a broad smile curving his sensuous lips. He slowly slides my underwear down my legs, then covers me with his body. His weight is heavy but comforting somehow. *I am ready for this.* For a moment, his mind goes elsewhere, and I wonder where his mind drifted off to. I feel his length sliding inside me, inch by inch, until his entire manhood is deep inside me.

"Does it hurt?" he whispers, peppering my face with light kisses.

Chills run up my spine, and I shake my head. He moves slowly, carefully at first, and then harder, faster, deeper. The sensations I feel overwhelm me, and my body quivers, gradually increasing until I am shaking. I throw my head back, my eyes closed, seeing stars. As I descend back to earth, I open my eyes and meet Kevin's. A sexy grin hovers on his lips as he watches me reach my pinnacle. Then he begins to move, and I feel the sensation growing within me again. When Kevin climaxes, our gazes are locked together, and

SEVENTEEN

I feel complete as I achieve my second orgasm. I don't want this moment to end.

Chapter 10

Depression in Session

WHAT JUST HAPPENED? *I lost my virginity to the hottest guy in my school, and he said he loved me.* I am floating on Cloud 9, reminiscing about everything that transpired between Kevin and me. He had grabbed me, placed me on his bed, and kept his eyes locked on mine the entire time. My heart races as I think about it. *It is getting hot in here!* I fan myself as I think about how sexy, loving, and caring he is, not to mention he knows how to pleasure me. There is no way Kevin can be the murderer that Eli claims.

While he sleeps, I study him in awe. I am in love with Kevin Evans, and I trust him completely. What happened last night was meant to be. But although my feelings for Kevin are strong, I can't help but feel an attraction toward Eli. When he touches me, electricity vibrates throughout my entire body as if our connection goes beyond the physical, and our magic completes one another. *Perhaps we're connected on a magical level, and that's it?*

I get out of bed and head to the bathroom to shower. Today I have a session with Ms. Hudson, and afterward, I will meet with the Witch Council since I've decided to keep my magic.

I haven't seen my father since the fight with the twins; I don't trust him, and now that I know what I know, he shouldn't have married that evil woman. I don't want to be around her or the vile twins, not with my magic developing. I don't know what I would do to one of them.

By the time I finish, Kevin is awake and in the kitchen, fixing breakfast in his boxers. *Why does he do this to me?* Kevin hands me a plate of eggs with a huge smirk. I lean in for a kiss, and he lifts me off my feet and places me on the counter, and we're going at it.

"Come on; I have to go, babe," I say between kisses.

"Let me have you."

"You already did."

He kisses my neck, and I melt into his arms. I do not want to leave, but I need to get to my session.

"Babe, I have to go. I'll see you tonight," I promise.

He accepts defeat, kisses me on the forehead, and retreats to the table to eat breakfast. Kevin had offered to let me use his car, so I grab his keys and head to my appointment.

Once I get to Ms. Hudson's house, she is remarkably cheerful. She seems in great spirits, but why?

"Hi Claudette, I heard the great news!" she exclaims.

"What do you mean? What good news have you heard?" I raise an eyebrow. *I'm pretty sure my losing my virginity wouldn't be a topic of discussion.* I walk into her office, sit on the sofa, and stare at Ms. Hudson; my head cocked, brow furrowed. *What has she heard?*

"I heard you accepted your magic." She beams at me, her eyes shining.

Oh, that's what she heard. Duh, Claudette!

I glance around the room at all the moon imagery. "I am going to go out on a limb and say you are a Moon witch?" A smile plays around my lips.

"Well, yes, of course. How would you have guessed?" She

chuckles. "Is it because of all of my moons?"

"I would believe so, Ms. Hudson," I reply deadpan.

She laughs, then sits and pulls out her small notebook from a desk drawer. "So, how are you feeling today?"

I feel amazing! "I am doing okay."

"Last time we were together, you discussed your mother, the move here, and your step-siblings." She flips a page, making a note. "I would like to discuss your stepsisters further if you don't mind."

"Um... sure." I shrug.

"How do you feel about them?" She studies me, eyes wide, pen poised, ready to write.

"They have been cruel to me since I first met them," I reveal.

"I see. Let me ask you this. Why do you think they have been harsh towards you?"

"Um... I don't know. Maybe because they are useless, pathetic, worthless sacks of rotten potatoes."

She scribbles in her notebook. My description of the twins might be a bit much, but I seriously can't stand them!

"Tell me about the first time you met the twins."

I huff. *I don't know why we need to discuss this.* "It was awful. I didn't know Gabriella was going to introduce them that night. It was supposed to be ice cream with just my father, but the third wheel, Gabriella, crashed our father-daughter date, and she brought the demon twins along." I scowl as I recall the memory.

Ms. Hudson nods and, of course, writes some more.

What is she writing about me in that notebook?

"Do you know the history of the twins and their father?"

"Yes, their father left them when they were babies."

"I see, and when you first met the twins, you were at an ice cream shop with your dad," she says.

"Yes, Dad and I went to Evi's three times a week. It was our ritual. You know, 'us time' until they ruined it." I fold my arms and stare out the window, my brows knitted. I never asked for a stepmother or stepsisters. My father should have asked if that was something I wanted, but then again, my mother was dead, and he was lonely. Suddenly, rage emerges from deep within me, and the room shakes.

"What is upsetting you, Claudette?" Ms. Hudson probes.

I don't respond. The lamp on her desk rocks back and forth and then plummets to the floor, shattering.

"Oh my! I'm so sorry! Please forgive me." I rush to pick up the pieces.

"It's okay. Leave it." Ms. Hudson waves her hand in a circular motion, fixing the lamp.

"Did the twins know about you and your father's ice cream dates?" she asks once the lamp is back in place.

"Yeah, they knew. I told them about it."

"I am not excusing their behavior, but you said their father left when they were babies. Then they meet a new father figure with a close relationship with his daughter. You have daddy-daughter dates, something they don't have with their father. Maybe they were cruel to you because they were jealous of your relationship with your father," she says. "And maybe you partially despise them for having a mother."

I swallow the lump forming in my throat. I never considered the twins could be jealous of my relationship with my father. But then, that's still no excuse to treat me the way they have this entire time. And okay, maybe I held something against them because their mom was still alive and mine was not.

"What you're implying is that they were jealous of my relationship with my father? What about making fun of my skin color? What was the point of that?"

"Yes, that is possible. Sometimes we must make connections to determine why people act as they do. Perhaps witnessing how close you are with your father stimulates uncomfortable feelings for them, and they don't know how to process it, so they treat you the way they do," she says. "Now, regarding your skin color. Some people are mean, or maybe they wish their skin was darker. So, they make fun of you for having something they wished they did. What you have to work on is how you respond." She closes her notebook and replaces it in the drawer. "Anytime you need to talk, I am here for you. I also spoke to your father. You should call him."

We say goodbye, and I consider her words as I leave her office and sit in the car for about fifteen minutes, processing our session. I wish the twins and I had a better relationship, but we have so much bad blood. I am at the point where I don't want to be bothered with them. Sometimes they make me feel so low that I no longer want to live. Perhaps it would be better if I left; they could have my father all to themselves. They made it clear from the first day we met they did not want me in this family.

I attempted suicide twice, and both times were unsuccessful. The first time I wanted to end it all was the day of my mom's death anniversary. I was in English class, and it was my turn to read aloud. I had been thinking about my mom, so I stuttered as I read. Marissa called me out in front of the entire class, saying I was "too stupid to read." Then at lunchtime, she stuck her foot out and tripped me, causing me to drop the tray I carried. The food ended up all over me, and Marissa laughed, pointing at me and calling me names.

I couldn't hold back my tears as she and all the other kids made fun of me, and when they saw me crying, they laughed more. I had wanted that day to be over; it was one of the worst ever.

As soon as we got home, I ran to my room and cried for hours.

My dad was working late, so I snuck out and took my bike for a ride. I rode through our neighborhood and headed to the train tracks. I thought that day would be my last. My school and home life sucked, and I missed my mother. *God! I missed my mom so much!* It had only been a few months since the twins and Gabriella had moved in with us, but I wanted them to leave from the beginning. *I would not have to deal with these demons if my mother was still alive!* I got off my bike and waited for the train to come.

I planned to jump in front of it and join my beautiful mother in the afterlife. When I heard the horns signaling the train was on its way, I walked toward the track and took a deep breath. This was it; I was ready to die. I did not feel anxious as I expected; I imagined how it would feel to be at peace finally and reunited with my mother. I was sure my father would miss me, but he had his new wife, Gabriella, and two new daughters. He did not need me. I stood there waiting for my end as I watched the bright white lights approaching me at full speed. I closed my eyes. *"Mom, I am on my way,"* I whispered.

Suddenly, the tracks changed, and the train went in a different direction. I was stunned. I had thought this was it, but somehow, I was saved. I fell to the ground in tears, wanting to die and for my life to end. *Why, why, why did this happen?* I used to think that maybe my mother had saved me and that she was my guardian angel. Maybe there is a reason I am supposed to be here; perhaps there was a reason I must suffer the way I have.

Tears flow down my face as I reminisce about the first time I attempted suicide. My father materializes in my thoughts, and I dry my eyes. I take out my phone to send him a text message. He is the only family I have. There was no reason I should not be talking to him. Ms. Hudson is right; I need to speak to Dad. But there is one thing I am very sure about—I do not want to be in the same house as his wife and stepdaughters, but I want to maintain a relationship with my father.

Me: We need to talk.

Dad: Whenever you're ready, Cheetah. I miss you!

Me: I miss you too. I'll call you tomorrow to set up a date.

Dad: Should we go to Evi's for ice cream?

Me: I would love that!

Feeling overwhelmed with emotions, I check my reflection in the mirror. There are tear stains on my face, and I wipe the running eyeliner underneath my eyes. I suck in air, slowly exhale, start the car, and head to the Witch Council meeting.

Chapter 11

The Council

WHEN I ARRIVE for my meeting with the Witch Council, my first impression of the building is that it looks like an ancient castle and is very creepy. It has the school's logo, the Sun, Moon, and Earth plastered everywhere. A woman is there to greet me but does not give me her name. She nods and gestures for me to follow her. As I walk through the building, there are portraits of all the council members throughout history hanging on the walls with small, gold plates underneath indicating the type of witch they were, Sun, Moon, or... I notice there aren't any Earth witches in the mix. *Hmm. I wonder why?*

"Have a seat." The tall woman points to a foldable black chair. She is brown-skinned and looks familiar. I am unsure where I have seen her before, but I know I have. Sensing movement out of the corner of my eyes, I turn and see Ms. Hudson entering. Her face is stern as she pulls a witch-like cloak over her shoulders. Three males, followed by Tanya and Tristan, walk behind her, slipping on similar robes as they move. *What type of cult mess have I gotten myself dragged into?*

"Hello Claudette, follow us," a tall, green-eyed man commands.

I do not want to follow them into the next room, but what can I do? We walk into what seems to be a large ballroom, which is odd. *What is this place?* A large table in the middle of the room has six oversized throne-like chairs, and they all sit down. *I guess Ms. Hudson is not my therapist right now. She is some weird cult lady leader.* The tall woman takes a long sheet of paper that looks like an old document off the table.

"My name is Elizabeth Powers, Claudette. We are here today to discuss your acceptance of magic."

Powers? Eli's mother!

"This is my husband Joseph and my older son Jeremiah; I am a Sun witch, and my husband and son are Moon witches. This is Jimmy; he is a Sun witch, and I am sure you already know Tanya and Tristan are Sun witches as well," she continues.

"And you already know I am a Moon witch," Ms. Hudson says.

"We need to discuss what it means for you to have power and the rules and consequences. You are not to use your magic on norms, use magic on mags, or harm anyone. You will begin magic classes on Monday to learn how to control your powers. Humans may not know of our existence, and your out-of-town friends may not visit here. Our town is cloaked from the outside world."

Blah blah blah... I zone out as Mrs. Powers drones on. She could have emailed me the rules so I wouldn't have to stand here, listening to her squeaky voice. I haven't heard a word she says after 'our town is cloaked,' which is pretty cool and weird, but I nod. It explains why we could not locate it on Google maps.

"Would you like to join the council as our first Earth witch?" The woman's voice breaks into my reverie.

For what? I am pretty sure my response should be no. "What does a council member do?" I ask, pursing my lips together.

"We look after the magical community and make sure that no

one misuses magic," Elizabeth says.

Sounds like something I don't need to be a part of. "I see. Well, this is a lot to take in, Mrs. Powers. I will have to get back to you if that's okay," I reply.

"Please respond in a reasonable time frame; the offer won't last," she hisses.

Rude much? I nod and bow because I do not know what else to do.

"You're excused." She gestures for me to leave the room like I am bothering her.

Wow, this was a bit much. Eli's mother was rude, and Mr. Powers and Eli's brother didn't even acknowledge I was in the room. Ms. Hudson was way too serious. Jimmy gave me a friendly smirk, and Tanya and Tristan nodded. I guess they are more serious at a council meeting than at school.

I get in the car and start the engine. When I am about to pull off, a pale woman with dark hair walks up to the vehicle, gesturing for me to roll down the window. I cannot make out her face.

"Hi, can I please talk to you?" she mouths, pointing to the window.

I do not want to, but I open it.

"Hello, Claudette. It's nice to meet you," she whispers.

I look to see if anyone else is around, confused, trying to figure out how she knows my name. I don't say anything.

"I'm Kevin's mother." Her voice is shaky.

Ah, now it makes sense. "Hello, nice to meet you," I say, eyeing her warily.

"You cannot trust Kevin!" she declares, then disappears into smoke.

That was vague and peculiar. But this is Kevin's *mother* saying that her own son cannot be trusted. Not knowing what to think, I sit there for a long moment, staring, unseeing, where she disappeared before finally pulling myself together and driving off.

Eli says I cannot trust Kevin. Isabel dislikes him, and now his mom says not to trust him. It does not look too good for Kevin. What am I supposed to believe?

As I drive, my mind races. It's really odd. Kevin's mom, whom I have never met, appears out of thin air, tells me her son is untrustworthy, then disappears.

I pull up at Kevin's place and sit in the car for about five minutes before heading inside. I feel like I should say something to him, but I bury the thought for now. I get out of the car and stride up the walkway. Taking a deep breath, I insert the key into the brass keyhole and enter the apartment. Kevin, wearing slacks and a button-up shirt, is preparing dinner. *How does he have me swooning even when I'm supposed to be suspicious of him?*

"Hey babe, how was your meeting with the Witch Council?" He smiles.

"It was... interesting." I stretch out the word, placing the keys on the holder. Whatever he's cooking smells scrumptious. *I swear he spoils me.*

"What are you making?" I stand over the stove, going through the pots and pans.

"Nothing special, just steak skirts, mashed potatoes, and asparagus." He opens the pantry closet to take out a bouquet of roses and hands them to me. "Go get dressed. I got you something special for our date night." He beams.

What?! I hurry to the bedroom to find a red-lace strapless gown on the mattress. I am in awe.

Kevin is one of those trust funds kids. His parents may not be on the Witch Council anymore, but he told me his father is a judge, and his mom is one of the best plastic surgeons in this town. So they have money! If he had accepted his magic, he could conjure anything he wanted. But there are rules and limits to materialistic items.

I undress and head to the bathroom to shower for our "date night." Once out of the shower, I place my "sister locks" into a bun and apply mascara to my eyelashes, a little reddish eyeshadow, and my favorite Maybelline eyeliner. I grab my red mat lipstick and roll it onto my lips to finish my look. I stand in front of the mirror, display my best vogue poses, then head to the dining area.

I can still hear Kevin's mother telling me Kevin is untrustworthy, but I push it to the back of my mind.

"You spent one hundred years in there." He fixes our plates of food.

"To be fair, you look hot and sexy, and I wanted to match you," I retort. "And thank you, babe, for my beautiful dress."

"You look amazing in it." He grins.

"Where did you get it?"

"I asked Tanya to conjure it for me." He beams.

"Oh, and here I thought you used some of that trust fund money to buy it." I giggle.

"I use that money for the mortgage. But very funny," he replies deadpan.

We begin eating, and the food is terrific; *my man sure knows how to cook.* We chit-chat about our day. I tell him about my therapy session, and he tells me about his time at the gym and how he and his brother seem on better terms now. I want to ask him about his relationship with his mom, but I do not want to ruin the moment.

He gets up to grab my favorite ice cream, butter pecan, from the freezer and gestures for me to join him on the sofa for a movie. Before it starts, he tells me that afterward, we will meet with Tristan and Tanya to witness a shooting star, which should be magical.

Just when the movie is about to start, I receive two text messages back-to-back. Glancing at the phone, I see they are from Eli. I do not open his messages because I notice Kevin watching me intently.

I turn my phone off, push it between the sofa cushions, and snuggle into Kevin's arms to enjoy a romantic comedy he picked out.

After the movie, I dart to the bathroom to check my phone to see what Eli wanted. I need to be quick because we're heading out to meet Tanya and Tristan.

Eli: Hey, can we talk?

Eli: Are you ignoring me?

Eli: I can't be the only one feeling this. You had to have felt that energy between us...

Eli: I would like for us to be friends, at least.

Seriously, dude? I text him, saying I will talk to him in school on Monday; I don't want to ruin the rest of my date night with my boyfriend.

Yes, I cannot deny that I felt something special when Eli and I touched; I also felt this strange sensation when we kissed. Our magic is definitely connected. However, I am in a relationship with a charming, handsome, and thoughtful guy who even cooks for me. Kevin has been so kind to me since we met; he has not given me a reason to distrust him. Of course, I trust him, although I can't fight this nagging feeling that I might need to meet with his mother again.

Welcome to the West Side

MASHAL HIGH

Classes for the Mags

- History of Magic–Taught by Mr. Goatfair
Where do Sun, Moon, and Earth witches come from?
- Potion Measurements–Taught by Ms. Caron
The right ingredients to use in a potion.
- Magical Elements–Taught by Mr. Max
How to harness your powers from the Sun, Moon, or Earth.
- Advanced Practical Magic–Taught by Ms. Billie
Spells, potions, and all things magic.

Chapter 12

Meet the Mags

WHEN I ARRIVE at school, I head straight to Principal Deanwall's office. Once there, he hands me a pamphlet with my classes and the instructors. I patiently wait for my first-period teacher to meet with me. I jiggle my leg and fidget in my chair. Of course, I am behind. I check my phone and see a text message from my father wishing me good luck. It is pretty much my first day all over again, except this time with magic. I text my dad to set our date for Wednesday after my therapy session, and he agrees. I have never gone this long without seeing my father, and it is time we made up. He is my only family, and it does not feel right for us to be at odds. It was against the rules for him to have told me about my magical ancestry, and I know it was not my parents' fault. They gave up their magic, and even if my mother had survived the heart attack, I don't think I should have known I was a witch.

Suddenly, a blonde-haired biker chick walks in, carrying a binder. Her eyes are blue-green, and she wears skinny black jeans and a leather jacket. A black streak running through her hair gives her a no-nonsense look. "Hi, you must be Claudette," she says, shifting her weight from one leg to the other as she aggressively chews on a piece of gum.

"Yes, nice to meet you." I extend my hand to shake hers.

She glares at my hand, then opens her binder. "My name is Ms. Billie. Do the work I give you, and we will be cool! Got it? Great!" she says, not giving me a chance to respond.

I nod, taking several sheets of paper she hands me and hurrying behind as she heads out of the office to a classroom.

There are illustrations of the Sun, Moon, and Earth on one wall. I feel awkward as all eyes are on me and keep my head down as I sit at the back of the room.

"Alright, class! Listen up; in today's lesson, we will focus on potions," Ms. Billie announces.

Most of the kids snap their fingers, and notebooks and pens appear. One kid is texting, ignoring Ms. Billie. She takes out a brown, gold, and black ancient-looking book from her black and silver bag and drops it on her desk with a resounding *thud*, which catches the kid's attention briefly. I lean in to get a closer look at the book and notice a Sun logo on the cover. It makes more sense now why our uniforms have a Sun, Moon, and Earth logo; they represent the different witch covens.

"Hey! Peanut head, get off your phone!" Ms. Billie snaps her fingers, and the student's phone turns into a flopping goldfish.

"Ms. Billie, why did you do that?" the kid whines, waving his hand to create a water bubble for the fish.

"Because I need your undivided attention!" she snaps.

The kid rolls his eyes, manifesting a notebook and pen on the desk before him.

"Okay, now that I have *everyone's* attention, let's get started! Claudette, take out your notebook unless you have a photographic memory." She gives me a grin.

Dumfounded, I pull a notebook and pen from my bag. Ms. Billie turns to the whiteboard and writes, "VANITY SPELL."

"Today, we will learn a simple vanity spell. Claudette, I will give a quick review; try to keep up! Sun witches are most powerful during the day, Moon witches are most powerful at night, and Earth witches are powerful whenever their little heart desires." She fixes her eyes on mine.

"Today, we are going to discuss healing yourself. If you were... let's say, in the middle of a battle, and your opponent inflicts pain on you, the only way you could heal yourself is if you drank *this*." She points to a small bottle of liquid. "This would heal any wound you incurred. As you all know, Ms. Caron will be the one to teach you about the ingredients needed for this potion."

I slowly raise my hand, and, of course, everyone turns to look. I do not want the spotlight on me, but I am taking this class to learn and have a question. But I immediately regret it once the question leaves my lips. "Do Earth witches have to use a potion to heal themselves?"

I feel it is a valid concern. I also want to know if I am just a typical witch or unique in some way, as Kevin and Eli seem to think.

"All witches have to use a potion to heal themselves," she says.

I must have made a face because suddenly she is standing next to me, studying me like I am some superhuman from a Marvel comic book.

"Did you heal yourself without a potion?" she asks.

"Yes," I say slowly, unsure if I should have mentioned it.

There is a resounding gasp throughout the classroom, and everyone gapes at me. Ms. Billie returns to her desk, types in a code, and pulls out a dagger. I get to my feet, frightened, and back away.

"Don't worry; if I were going to kill you, I would have done it already." She chuckles.

What kind of teacher would tell a student if they wanted to

murder you, they would?

She strides toward me. "Stay calm. I am just going to cut you to see for myself."

I'm sorry, what?

"Oh, no, you're not!" I shout.

She glances toward the window, closes her eyes, and takes a deep breath. Suddenly, I freeze in place, unable to move.

"I am going to scream. You can't do this!" The only part of me I can move is my lips.

"Calm down, Claudette. I am in the middle of teaching a lesson, and I need you to cooperate!" Ms. Billie uses the dagger to pierce my right hand, and blood trickles from the cut. I try to move, but I can't.

"What is wrong with you, lady?" I yell.

The class chuckles, amused by my pain.

"Heal yourself!" she commands.

When I can move, I hold my hand in agony. I glance at my classmates, hoping and wishing I could see Eli. He was the one who had made me feel confident enough to heal myself before. I do not know if I can do it without him.

"Heal yourself," Ms. Billie repeats.

I close my eyes, inhale deeply, then breathe out slowly. A marching band stomps inside my head as my heart races to the beat of the drums. I do not know how I will do it. I can hear Eli's soothing voice telling me to heal myself, and the cut suddenly disappears. The students gasp in unison, and Ms. Billie regards me with wide eyes. She darts to the front of the class, grabs her cell phone, and exits the room. I feel like a fish out of water trying to find my way to the nearest ocean. The bell rings, and thankfully, this class is over. It is time for the next, but Ms. Billie does not return to dismiss us.

My next class is Potion Measurements, taught by Ms. Caron. As I walk there, I spot Ms. Billie whispering to another teacher. When she notices me, she turns her back. I shrug it off and enter the class, shuffling my way to the back of the room to avoid being the center of attention again. I notice Isabel and Destiny walk in, holding hands. A smile forms on my face; they are the first familiar faces I've seen today. I also notice Lin, who gives me a nod, and to sweeten the deal, I see Eli enter. *I thought he was a no-show today.* I smile and wave at him, but he does not acknowledge me. *Ouch!* I take out my phone and text him because I do not want anyone to overhear.

Me: Are you giving me the silent treatment now?

Eli: You made it clear how you felt.

Me: I am sorry that you don't trust my boyfriend.

Eli: Don't be. I will talk to you after class.

I growl and throw my phone in my bag with force. Like he did not give me any proof that my boyfriend was a murderer. When you accuse someone of murder, you should have evidence to back it up. I questioned Kevin about Eli's allegations; he said he hadn't killed anyone. I believed him. *Hmm. Didn't his mother say not to trust him?* a voice inside my head says. I am conflicted. I trust Kevin, but I also trust Eli. Maybe it's because Eli has feelings for me that he doesn't trust Kevin. *But why accuse him of murder? That is overboard.*

Ms. Caron glides into the classroom, eyes fixed on me. She is light-skinned with light brown eyes and burgundy curls. She looks familiar, but I cannot place where I have seen her before.

"Hello, class. Please take out your cauldrons. We will prepare a truth potion today," she announces in her husky voice.

Everyone's interest has peaked, and some look worried.

"Guys, please pick a partner." Ms. Caron walks to her closet and gets me a cauldron.

"Thank you," I say as she hands it to me, and she gives me a small smile.

She walks back to her closet and takes out the ingredients for the potion. I glance around at the other students as they pair up. Of course, Destiny and Isabel are partners. Eli, myself, and Lin are left. Just as I am about to ask Lin to be my partner, Eli pulls his desk next to mine.

"You're mine," he declares in a deep, husky voice.

"I'm sorry... yours?" I raise an eyebrow. "So you're not giving me the silent treatment anymore?"

"My partner is what I meant... and obviously not." A charming smile curves across his lips and makes my stomach flutter.

"Lin, please help me hand out the ingredients," Ms. Caron says.

He hands Eli and me ginger, burdock root, two cups of water, a mint leaf, and what looks like a piece of a brain. I lean in and whisper to Eli, asking him if it is a human brain, and he nods. *Gross! I wonder what poor soul they used for this!*

"Humans donate their brains for this very purpose." Eli grazes his hand over mine. *It is as if he can hear what I am thinking.* Shock waves transfer from his touch through my hand, up my arm, until I feel it in my chest. For a moment, I cannot breathe. My heart is racing so fast that I am sure I will need to see a cardiologist to regulate it again. As much as I do not want to admit it, there is something between Eli and me that Kevin and I do not have. The energy between us every time we touch is transcending.

"Eyes up front!" Ms. Caron demands, bringing us back to reality. "Please, I want you all to add one cup of water into your cauldrons, followed by two ounces of ginger, four ounces of burdock root, a mint leaf, and finally, the most important ingredient, three tablespoons of the human brain." She cackles, sounding like an evil witch. "This is my favorite part!" She stirs the ingredients together.

"You guys should work on your laughs while doing this."

I glance at Destiny with a worried expression, who mouths, "She is just joking."

"Let the liquid cool for about five minutes before pouring it into your vials," Ms. Caron instructs.

I watch her before stirring mine because I want to pay close attention to what she is doing, but I cannot take my mind off the connection between Eli and me. *I wish I had met him first.*

The feelings I have are confusing. I love Kevin, and he treats me wonderfully, but Eli is just as sweet, and we have this undeniable connection.

"Now it's time to test it out on your partner; please allow five minutes for the potion to take effect. Once processed, the potion will last only five minutes," Ms. Caron announces.

While I let my potion cool, Eli pours his into the bottle. He takes out a piece of paper and scribbles.

"What are you writing?" I question, eyes wide, trying to look over his shoulder.

"I am writing questions for you to ask me," he says.

Once my potion is cool, I pour it into a small bottle and cork it.

"So, should I go first, or would you like to?" I ask, biting my lip.

He places his hand on me, sending shocks throughout my body.

"You really need to stop doing that!" I exclaim.

"I'll go first," he offers.

He opens the potion and guzzles it down. I turn the timer on and wait precisely five minutes before I ask my first question, ignoring the list he gave me.

"What is happening between us when you touch me?"

"Our energy is connecting," he replies immediately.

But how do I know if it's working? "How do I know if the potion is working on you?"

"If you look me in the eye, you will see I am not blinking," he says robotically.

I look around at everyone in the classroom, and it is as if they are all hypnotized as they answer the questions asked by their partners. I only have a few more minutes, so I want to ask a more serious question.

"What is your issue with Kevin?"

"Kevin is evil and cannot be trusted."

"Are you just saying that because you have feelings for me?" I press.

"No, I am your soulmate. Not Kevin."

"What do you mean by *soulmate*?" I arch an eyebrow.

"Sorry, you will just have to find that out later." He smirks.

The spell is over, and Eli is officially out of the trance. The bell rings, and it is time for my next class.

"Eli, seriously?" I say.

"Claudette, I get it. You're in a relationship with Kevin and trust him. But when he ultimately breaks your heart... and trust me, he will. I will be here to pick up the pieces." He hands me my books.

I do not know what to say. Yes, I feel connected to Eli, but I am in a relationship and unwilling to let that go. Even though something is spurring between Eli and me, I do not want to explore it. It is best to keep things strictly platonic—*because of Kevin*. I grab my bag and head to my next class, which I do not have with Eli. They shuffle us between the four magical classes, so Eli and I only have two subjects together. I cannot stop thinking about his words as we head in opposite directions. *We are soulmates*. I mean, I am seventeen years old. How would I know who my soulmate is?

My day continues smoothly, and I enjoy learning about magic more than I thought I would. *Becoming a mag is one of the best decisions I have ever made.*

SEVENTEEN

I spend my lunch hour with Destiny, Isabel, Lin, and Eli. Usually, I have lunch with Kevin, but he left school early today because he was not feeling well. I call to check on him when school ends, and he tells me he feels worse.

Destiny gives me a ride "home"–well, to Kevin's apartment. When I get there, he does not look well. I prepare some soup for us, and after looking over a few spell books, we head to bed early.

Kevin is too sick to attend school the following day, so I ask Isabel to pick me up. Ms. Billie cancels classes for the rest of the week for some unknown reason, but I am pretty sure it has something to do with me. My other classmates gossip about me healing myself without a potion, and I am the talk of Mashal High School. The twins are avoiding me, and it is lovely. When they see me walking down the hallway, they turn around and walk in the opposite direction, avoiding me like the plague.

My classes seem to drag on for the rest of the day, and although the courses are much more interesting, there is still much information to cram for one day. I am mentally drained after school, and Kevin and I crash when I get home.

When Wednesday comes around, Kevin is still not feeling well. After school, Isabel drops me back at the apartment, so I can get Kevin's car to drive to my therapy session at six-fifteen. Our session is only twenty minutes today because I want to meet my father by six-forty. I plan to head to the house to meet him there, and then we'll drive to our old town and have ice cream at Evi's. I have not spoken to Nicolette and Spencer since before my birthday, and they stopped reaching out to me after I did not respond to a few of their text messages. I send them a text while waiting for Ms. Hudson to arrive.

Me: Hey guys, I am so sorry I have been MIA. I learned a lot about my history, and I can't tell you until it is safe. I want you

both to know I love you and will fill you in soon.

Spencer: CLAUDETTE! It's great to hear from you finally. Please tell us what's going on!

Nicolette: You have some explaining to do!

Me: I promise I will explain everything to you guys. When I can.

It is against the rules to inform humans about magic, but I must tell them. They are my two best friends. I know they won't tell anyone.

I glance at my watch when I realize that Ms. Hudson is still not here. Looking at my phone again, I notice I had somehow missed a voicemail from her saying she was running late. I call Kevin to check on him, and he does not answer. Perhaps he is sleeping. While sitting in the throne-like chair, waiting for Ms. Hudson to arrive, I text Eli to see what he is doing. But he does not respond either.

"Hi, Claudette. I apologize for my tardiness," Ms. Hudson says as she rushes in.

"No worries," I reply, following her into the office.

As I sit down, I look at her closely. She seems flushed, like she has been doing something. She stares out the window. I follow her gaze and see an older gentleman outside. He winks at Ms. Hudson, and she blushes.

Was she late because she was getting some? Eww. Ms. Hudson smiles and waves at the man.

"Today's session will be short, and I apologize for being late. It is very unprofessional of me," she says.

"Is that your guy?" I incline my chin toward the window. She smiles but does not respond.

"Claudette, how was your day?" she asks instead.

"It was great. I'm managing my magic better, with fewer outbursts, and who knew witches were so fascinating? My relationship with Kevin is great. The twins are avoiding me. Gabriella doesn't bother me anymore, and I am supposed to meet my father today after this session for an ice cream date." I grin from ear to ear.

"Oh, that is awesome! So, let me ask, when do you plan to return home for good?"

"I don't think living there is best for me; I will be cordial, but living under the same roof as my stepmother and stepsisters is a huge no."

"Okay, I get that. And there is nothing wrong with not wanting to be around them. And it's great that you are going out with your father later. You guys need your daddy-daughter one-on-one time." Ms. Hudson scribbles down a few words in her notebook and tells me to work on gradually getting in one-on-one time with my father every week. I agree, and we part ways. Then I head to my dad's house.

After so long, I am looking forward to seeing him again. I give Kevin another call, but he still doesn't answer. *I hope he is okay.* I arrive at my father's house and ring the doorbell. When he does not answer, I get the spare key underneath the mat and let myself in. My dad informed me about the spare key underneath the rug when Kevin gave my key back for me. I open the door and enter, checking the kitchen first, but Dad's not there, so I run upstairs.

"Dad, are you here?"

There's still no sign of him. I go to check the den next and find my father lying on the floor in a pool of blood.

Chapter 13

Why?

DISPATCHER: 911, what's your emergency?

Me: My father! My father is not breathing!

Dispatcher: Okay, I need you to calm down. Please tell me your name.

Me: My name is Claudette. Please help me!

Dispatcher: Okay, Claudette. I will help you. Where are you located?

Me: 1103 TK Avenue.

Dispatcher: Claudette, put the phone on speaker and listen carefully.

Me: Okay.

Dispatcher: Seal your mouth over your father's and blow steadily and firmly into his mouth for about one second. Can you do that for me?

Me: Uh-huh.

Dispatcher: Check to see if his chest is rising. If so, continue with cycles of thirty chest compressions and two rescue breaths until help arrives.

Me: Mm-hmm.

Dispatcher: Alright, Claudette, help will be there soon. Keep it steady... okay?

Me: Mm-hmm.

Dispatcher: I will stay on the line until help arrives.

So many thoughts reel through my mind as I try to bring my father back. *What happened? Where are Gabriella and the twins? Why is this happening?*

"Please, daddy, come back to me," I plead, tears flowing. *Wait, I am a witch!*

With my hands on his chest, I channel my energy into him, chanting, "Please wake up, please wake up, please wake up!"

But nothing happens. My heart is breaking; my face soaked with tears. What could have happened for my father to end up in a pool of blood? Did he fall and hit his head? I don't understand why this is happening. *He is the only family I have left!*

The paramedics bust through the door, and one pulls me to the side. I watch them work on my father for over twenty minutes, trying to bring him back. I stand there, wringing my hands, watching the chaotic scene unfold. It's as if I'm watching from afar. My heart squeezes in my chest, and my legs tremble. They can barely hold my weight, and I lean against the wall, not taking my eyes from my father, lying unconscious on the floor. When the paramedic announces, "*Call it... time of death,*" my legs give out, and I collapse. A loud wail fills the air, and after a moment, I realize the animalistic sound is coming from me.

My father is dead, and I am officially an orphan. Before the paramedics can place my father in a body bag, I lay my head on his chest, no longer hearing his thumping heart. My vision blurs, and I whimper silently. Clutching my father for one last hug, I stare at his beloved face through my tear-blurred eyes. That's when I notice he has something clenched in his fist.

SEVENTEEN

One paramedic steps forward, ready to take my father away.

"Please let me say goodbye to my father," I plead. The woman moves away, and I discreetly open Dad's fist to remove the object and slip it into my pocket. I kiss his forehead. "Goodbye, daddy," I whisper before getting up from the floor.

I call Kevin once more, but he still does not answer. My heart sinks. I need him so much right now. *Where is he?* I call Gabriella next, and then the twins, but no one answers my calls.

The paramedics roll the stretcher with my father out of the room. I cannot call Nicolette or Spencer because they will want to come here, but how could I explain to them it's against the rules? I scroll down my contact list, calling everyone I can think of, needing to talk to someone. I try Eli first, but the call goes straight to voicemail. Neither Destiny nor Isabel answer their phones. I know it's their date night, but I hoped they would pick up if they saw my back-to-back calls, getting the hint it's urgent.

The detectives walk in right after the paramedics and begin asking me questions. *Why are they here?* My mind spirals, and my throat is dry from all the crying, so my voice comes out hoarse when I speak. I do not know how to respond to the detectives' questions. They ask if anything is missing, and I recall noticing that my father wasn't wearing his Earth ring and necklace. The Earth ring makes sense now that I know about my magical heritage. Dad never took it off. When I tell the police about the missing jewelry, they immediately conclude this was a robbery "gone bad," in their words. They ask about my stepfamily, and I tell them I've been calling but have not gotten an answer. From what the detectives say, I realize they think Gabriella and the twins are suspects. *Suspects? Do they think someone killed my father?* Mashalville is a small town. Surely they will find the person who murdered my father if that's what happened. But then I remember the police have still not solved the murders of Destiny's mother and Isabel's parents.

I shudder and wrap my arms around myself. There is no way I am staying in this house, so I leave after checking with one detective that I am free to go. I do not know where to go; no one answers my calls. As I sit in the car, thinking, loneliness implements the worst ideas in my head. *Why is no one answering my calls? Where is everybody?* I punch the steering wheel, my jaw set, a fire blazing in my eyes. A burning fury swells inside me as my mind flips through potential suspects. Right now, I *can* trust no one. Not until I check alibis that prove they couldn't have killed my father. I decide on my next destination, start the engine, and head directly to Kevin's parents' house. *It's time to get to the truth.*

When I arrive at the house, I see Kevin's mother immediately—all the confidence I had while on the way here dissipates at the sight of her. I am about to pull away when his mother appears in the passenger's seat, making me gasp.

"Why are you here?" she whispers.

I grip the steering wheel until my knuckles turn white and take a few seconds to even my breathing before I can answer her. *It is now or never.* "I need to know why I can't trust your son," I say, my voice giving away none of the turmoil I feel.

"What has he told you?" She cocks her head to the side, fixing me with her eyes.

Kevin told me his parents are Sun witches, and their union is against the rules. Because they did not want to take the chance of him being evil, they took away his magic, preventing him from making a choice.

"He hasn't told me anything," I lie, and my head feels heavy. I just need answers without having questions shot at me.

"My son..." Her voice trails off, and she suddenly looks like she is in a daze.

I shift in my seat to face her. "What's wrong with you?"

"I am an empath, and your pain overwhelms me. I am so sorry for your loss."

"Thank you." I wave a hand dismissively, avoiding eye contact. I do not want her pity. What I want are answers. "What about Kevin? Please tell me why I can't trust your son! I am living with him!"

Someone has murdered my father, and even though I do not want to think about it, my boyfriend is a potential suspect. I want to clear his name to get rid of this disgusting thought.

"I am sorry I gave you that impression. Kevin is a fine man who loves you," she replies, her voice a monotone.

I notice her eyes are blank and watch in disbelief as she opens the door and walks away.

My phone rings, snapping my attention away from Kevin's mother, and I see Eli calling me back. I don't answer. Eli will have to wait until later when my mind is in a suitable space.

I head straight to Kevin's, intending to confront him. I need to know his mother's deal. *First, she tells me I can't trust Kevin, and now she says I can. I'm so confused.*

I hop out of the car, not even locking the door behind me, and storm inside. Before I can unleash my wrath, I see Kevin scrunched up in one corner of the kitchen floor, beaten. Immediately, concern replaces my anger.

"Oh, my God!" I rush to him. "Kevin! What happened to you?" I kneel on the floor beside him, stroking his face. Flashes of cradling my father in my arms earlier materialize as I hold Kevin, and I suck in air.

"Eli!" he whispers, bringing me back to the present.

"No, no, no, this is not true. He couldn't have done this to you. He wouldn't," I say. *Who am I trying to convince, him or myself?*

"He did this to me, Claudette. Why would I lie?" he weakly protests.

When I do not respond, Kevin struggles, trying to get up, but falls back down, and I steady him. "Stay away from Eli, Claudette. He is dangerous," he urges, pleading with his eyes.

I swallow hard and shake my head. "Eli is not dangerous," I say and help Kevin to his feet and into the bedroom. *Kevin can't be right about Eli, but why would he lie?* I bite my lip. This back-and-forth between us about Eli is an ongoing argument. Kevin is tired of me always defending Eli, taking Eli's side over his. And I am tired of the friction between the two of them. *But Kevin wouldn't lie.* I shake my head again. Whether in disagreement with the thought or to clear my mind, I don't know.

My phone rings as we enter the bedroom, and I help Kevin to the bed before answering. It's Gabriella, finally returning my call. I hear her screaming on the other end that someone has murdered my father. Kevin overhears, and I see his eyes widen, his mouth falling open.

Gabriella's reaction sounds sincere; I can hear the pain in her voice. She could not have murdered my father. She may hate me, but her love for my father is genuine.

When I hang up, Kevin is waiting for me to talk to him, but I rummage through the dresser, looking for something to wear, not saying anything. I am antsy and cannot stay still. My mind is running a mile a minute, and my body is trying to keep up. I am determined to find my father's killer, and, most importantly, I want to know *why. Why would someone kill Dad?* This town is so small. Whoever murdered my father could not have gone far—magic or no magic.

"Claudette, come here." Kevin pats the mattress beside him, breaking the silence.

I whirl around and glare at him. "No, Kevin! My father is dead. Somebody killed him. I am going to find out who."

My limbs feel weak, and my heart races. This is a nightmare I need to escape. "I can't right now. I just... can't."

He gets up, grunting from the pain, and shuffles toward me. He pulls me into his muscular frame, and I bury my face in his chest and sob uncontrollably as he rubs my back.

"I love you," Kevin whispers, and I weep even more. I feel broken and lost, completely and utterly devastated by my father's death. *Why did this happen?*

Kevin guides us to the bed, and we lie down. I cry for hours while he holds me, chanting sweet nothings in my ear until sleep claims me.

I wake up in the middle of the night in a panic from a nightmare. I glance at Kevin, but he is still asleep, so I pull on my robe and head to the kitchen to get a glass of water.

When I return to the bedroom, I grab my phone from the nightstand and see a few missed calls and a text message from Eli. By now, the news about my father's murder has spread. Kevin accusing Eli of beating him up resurfaces, and I step out of the bedroom to call Eli back to question him about what happened between them. He answers almost immediately, his voice sounding sleepy. When interrogating him, he tells me he has reason to believe Kevin is behind my father's death, and I hang up on him.

I feel sick to my stomach at his allegations against my boyfriend. I had doubted Kevin for a brief moment, but I could not have been more wrong. He has been nothing but supportive the entire time he has known me. Rage builds inside me, and I march to the bedroom to get dressed, inadvertently waking Kevin.

"Claudette, where are you going?" He sits up, rubbing his eyes.

"I need to clear my mind," I whisper. "Go back to sleep."

"Let the detectives do their job, baby. They will find out who killed your father," he assures me.

He gets out of bed and treads toward me, grasping my waist and running his fingers along my thigh. He presses his lips softly on my forehead, and I inhale his natural musk, temporarily feeling at ease.

I peer up at him, seeing his cut lip and swollen eye. I place my hand over his wounds and heal them.

He takes my hand and kisses it. By the look on his face, I can tell how thankful he is that I healed him.

"I love you, Claudette," he says.

"I love you, too," I say.

His lips touch mine, and the rage I feel fades away. I want to feel something other than this pain. I no longer wish to think about never seeing my father again. I wrap my arms around Kevin's neck, turning our passionate kiss into something more.

Kevin catches my drift and palms my breast softly, teasing me. "Babe, come back to bed."

I remove my pants and shirt and sit on the bed. Eyes fixed on mine, Kevin slips off my underwear and removes my bra, leaving me naked. Pushing me into the middle of the bed, he climbs on top of me. I can hear his heart racing.

"I wish I could take your pain away," he whispers. His warm breath on my earlobe sends my body into overdrive, and he knows it. I can feel his affection for me, and I do not want this moment to end. He removes his boxers, exposing himself to me, then inserts his hard length deep inside me. I moan. This was what I need to distract myself from my sorrow.

The following morning, I stagger to the bathroom. I awoke feeling refreshed after my night with Kevin, momentarily forgetting about yesterday's events, but reality slapped me in the face as soon as I regained consciousness.

I glance at myself in the mirror; my eyes are puffy and red from crying. I look like a blowfish. I put my hair in a bun, slip on sweatpants, leaving the apartment as quietly as possible. Kevin is sound asleep, so I use this opportunity to finally get to the bottom of the altercation between Eli and him.

Once outside, I three-way call Nicolette and Spencer and tell them everything, not only about Dad's murder but also about being a witch. I swear them to secrecy, telling them I will come to see them. I am sure Nicolette is questioning my sanity about my claims of being a witch, but I will prove it once I am with them. They need to know what happened, and I no longer care about the rules. The rules did not save my father.

I look up from my phone and see Eli's car pulling up. Parking, he quickly hops out of the car and approaches me. I cannot deny our magical connection because he appears with a mere thought.

"What did you do to Kevin?!" I demand.

He grasps me by the shirt and places his index finger over my lips. "Shh! Not here."

He snaps his fingers, and suddenly we are atop a mountain in the middle of nowhere. I break away from him, my heart slamming in my chest as I have no idea where we are. I inch away from him and look over the edge of the cliff. It's a long way down. Lifting my eyes, I survey the scenery. It's beautiful; the sunrise is stunning, and a cascading waterfall is a sight to behold. My eyes widen. *Why would Eli bring me here?*

"Claudette?" Eli whispers.

"*What?*" I yell, and my voice echoes.

"Kevin is up to some–"

I raise a hand, gesturing for him to stop.

"Wait, please hear me out. I brought you here because I made a truth potion for you. I need you to sneak and give it to Kevin. Ask him if he killed your father."

"You think Kevin murdered my dad?" I stare at him in disbelief. *Why am I surprised? Eli hates Kevin.* I roll my eyes. I do not have the energy for this.

"I am pretty certain he did," he says.

"*Pretty certain* and certain are two entirely different things, Eli! Pretty certain leaves room for innocence. Do you understand what you're insinuating?" I ground my jaw, seething.

Eli sighs. He places both hands on my shoulders and looks directly into my eyes. "Listen to me, Claudette. Kevin is close with Tristan and Tanya. They are from the same coven, are romantically involved, *and* are part of the Witch Council. The three of them are evil. Furthermore, there has been no sign of an Earth witch until *you*. Destiny told me that Kevin suddenly signed up to be an escort for new students when he found out that *you* were coming to this school. Why would I make this up?!" Eli gives me a little shake. "And before you answer, I know you think, or I'm assuming you think, I am not a fan of Kevin because I have feelings for you, but that's not it. He has something to do with your father's death, and I need you to trust me on this." He lets go of my shoulder and extends the potion to me. "Take this and ask him if he killed your father. I know you don't have feelings for me in that way, but I can't sit back and let you be lied to by the likes of him. If I'm wrong, I'll let it go."

I'm silent for a long moment, absorbing everything he says. "Eli, I'm sorry, but I trust Kevin," I say gently, choosing my words carefully. "And if we are to continue a friendship, I need you to stop this—*especially* now. I can't handle any more disappointments. I need you to be a friend." My voice quivers. I do not have the strength to continue this fight.

"Please, Claudette, take the potion. If he is telling the truth, I promise it will be the last you hear from me about it."

I sigh and take the potion, putting it in my pocket. Eli takes my hand, and instantly we are back at Kevin's apartment.

"Ask him," Eli mouths before heading back to his car.

I trudge back inside, my heart heavy, my mind drained. I do not want to believe my boyfriend could have committed such a heinous crime. There is no way he killed my father. He wasn't even feeling well. I would believe it was Gabriella, or even the twins, who murdered Dad before I thought Kevin had. But they were just as surprised as I was. When I spoke to Gabriella, I could tell she was genuine. My heart is pounding so hard I can feel it in my head. The air feels thinner, and the room spins. I feel weak and lightheaded like I'm ready to pass out. Kevin is charming, loving, sexy, and kind. *He couldn't have done this. Could he?* I take out the potion and stand there, staring at the bottle for a moment. Then, almost zombie-like, I move to the stove and put the teapot to boil. I don't feel like myself. I am about to break Kevin's trust, and it feels wrong. Yet, I continue.

Once the water boils, I take Kevin's favorite red mug and another one for me from the cupboard. Removing the stopper from the potion bottle, I stare at it again before pouring the contents into the red mug. I wait five minutes before heading into the room. Kevin is still asleep.

I shake him gently. "Babe, I made you some tea. Here, drink it."

Rubbing his eyes, he smiles sleepily. "Thank you, babe."

I blow on my tea and take a sip, studying Kevin from the corner of my eye. Knowing that the potion effects only last five minutes, I try to think of my questions and word them correctly.

"Why would Eli beat you up?" I ask.

"Because he hates me," he replies in a robotic tone.

The potion is working! "Did you kill my father?"

129

"No, I didn't," he says, tone still robotic. "Why are you asking me that?"

"Because Eli told me to ask you," I blurt out. I am not under the potion's effects, but it does not sit right with me lying to him.

Kevin eyes me warily. It is as if he knows he is under a spell.

The silence stretches between us, and I say, "Do you know who murdered my father?"

He hesitates for about two seconds before saying, "No."

When he hesitated, I was unsure if I could believe his response. I glance at my watch and see that over five minutes have passed. The potion's effects have worn off.

"Did you use magic on me?" Kevin stares at me. His voice sounds broken. I can tell it hurt him that I would use magic on him, knowing it is against the rules.

"I am sorry, Eli—"

Kevin cuts me off mid-sentence. "No, you don't need to explain. You lost your father. As far as I am concerned, everyone in this town is a suspect. We will get to the bottom of his murder," he promises, taking me into his muscular arms, and I could not have been more content with his response.

I snuggle deeper into Kevin's arms, drawing comfort from his warm embrace. Remembering my earlier conversation with Eli, a sudden thought hits me. Eli said he attacked Kevin because he thought Kevin had something to do with Dad's murder. But... *how did Eli know about my father's murder before we spoke?* I clench my jaw, my hands curling into fists. *I will find out who killed you, Dad. There are no lengths I will not go to, even if it means losing myself in the process. Your death will not go unavenged.*

End of Part I.

SEVENTEEN

Keep reading for a sneak peek at *Earth*. The next book in the Magic is Real series.

If you have enjoyed this story, please consider leaving a review on Amazon or your favorite online bookstore, Goodreads, BookBub, and any other online book review site you may visit frequently. Reviews are a great way to help readers discover new books and help Indie Author books become more visible. Also, when someone enjoys our stories, it pushes us to continue writing.

MAGIC IS REAL
PART II.

EARTH

K.C. MCMILLIAN

NOVELLA

Chapter 1

Confessions of a Teenage Witch

DEAR DIARY,

I am writing in this diary because Ms. Hudson advised that I use this as a coping mechanism to eliminate my aggression. I am debating whether transferring my thoughts onto paper will work, but I'll try. What do I have to lose?

It has been eight weeks since someone murdered my father, and the police still have not caught the person who did it.

Just like they swept Destiny's mother's and Isabel's parents' deaths under the rug, the police seem to have given up on solving my father's murder. I haven't attended school in over a week and don't eat or sleep. I keep thinking about who could have murdered my father and why? On that dreadful day my father died, he had something clenched in his fist. I retrieved it from his hand when the paramedics weren't looking and hid it in my pocket. It was a flash drive. I haven't looked at it yet because I am not ready to see what is on it, but I have it in a safe place. I don't care about anything other than finding out who murdered my father. But here's a turn of events. Gabriella calls me daily, and Kevin and I aren't on good terms.

The Witch Council summoned me for a meeting tomorrow because I told my friends about magic. What they don't know is my magic has grown over the weeks, so if they think I'll let them remove it, they can think again.

*****

"Good morning, Claudette," Kevin greets me as I walk to the sofa. "Do you plan on eating breakfast today—or ever?"

I don't look at him as I pick up the remote and flip through the channels. A few days after the funeral and my first phone call from Eli's irritating mother, I overheard Tanya and Tristan discussing the Witch Council's plan to remove my magic with Kevin, and he agreed with them. I know that telling my friends about magic was against the rules, but I hoped my *boyfriend* would support me no matter what. But apparently, he doesn't think I can control my emotions and believes I shouldn't possess such powers as a new witch. Since overhearing that conversation, our relationship has been on the rocks. The council, including Ms. Hudson, didn't approve of my two best friends accompanying me to the funeral, and now they want to take my magic away using a spell and a ceremonial knife known as a *"Ce-ja."* All because I took Kevin's car, drove to my old hometown to pick up my friends, and brought them to Mashalville for the funeral. I didn't care about the rules then, and I don't care about them now. I trust Nicolette and Spencer with my life—about the only two people I do trust—and I know they would never betray me.

"How long are you going to give me the silent treatment?" Kevin presses.

I snort. "Why should I talk to you?"

"What is your issue, Claudette?" He walks towards me cautiously.

"My issue? What. Is. My. Issue?" I spit out slowly through gritted teeth.

His lips twist into a frown, and I can tell he chooses his words carefully when he speaks. "Claudette, I know you miss your father. But this is not the way to act. I haven't done anything to you, and I can't help but think you're blaming me for something."

I throw my head back and descend into uncontrollable laughter. *Is he serious? He really doesn't know?*

"Really, Kevin? Are we going to pretend you don't know why I am upset? I know you were angry about my friends being here. Am I supposed to act as if I am okay with you siding with the Witch Council?" I hiss.

"Claudette, humans aren't supposed to know about magic! If that's why you're upset, I suggest you get over it! Because I am not changing my stance on it."

"Noted!" I jump to my feet, rushing out of the room. I get my already-packed bag from the closet and use my magic to take me to Eli's house. That argument was all I needed to solidify my decision to leave.

I understand the rules are there for a reason, and I get that just because I trust Nicolette and Spencer doesn't mean everyone else will or can. But how could they think I wouldn't want my two best friends from childhood to be by my side as I said goodbye to my father? I didn't tell them that the town was full of magic; I told them I had magic and that my mother had it. I also told them someone murdered my father, and no one in this god-forsaken town knows who! Yes, I revealed some secrets, but not all, and the fact my *"boyfriend"* can't be on my side is a deal breaker for me.

(A text message between Kevin and Tanya.)

Kevin: Hey, you need to locate Claudette. NOW! She just left, and I have no idea where she went.

Tanya: Are you serious? You were to watch her. What are we supposed to do now? The Witch Council wants to see her tomorrow.

Kevin: What do you expect me to do with no magic? She's powerful. You need to conduct the ceremony ASAP.

Tanya: You best pull out your charm and reel her back in.

Kevin: It's too late; she knows I've sided with the Witch Council to take her magic away. And I am tired of keeping up this facade.

Tanya: Stick to the plan, Kevin! We almost have what we want.

✶✶✶✶✶

If you enjoyed this story, please consider leaving a review on Amazon. Scan the QR code to go directly to the Amazon page. Reviews help other readers find good books!

✶✶✶✶✶

Stay tuned for *Earth*, "Magic is real" Part II. coming 2024, and the re-release of *Bright: A Forbidden Love Story* (Book One of the Bright Series), coming later this year!

AUTHOR'S NOTE

Thank you for purchasing this novella! I hope you have enjoyed my story as much as I enjoyed writing it.

Let's be friends!

I enjoy connecting with my readers and would love to hear from you. Who do you think killed Claudette's father? Please find me on any social media platforms below and let me know!

Instagram: www.instagram.com/kcminspired_author

Facebook: www.facebook.com/kcmcmillianauthor

TikTok: www.tiktok.com/@kcminspired_author

GR: www.goodreads.com/author/show/22481124.K_C_McMillian

ACKNOWLEDGMENT

I have learned a great deal from writing Seventeen. Putting a story on paper takes courage and determination. Writing this novella was challenging since I have two children under four and a full-time job. But I did it! The words of encouragement from others helped me through this process. I wrote this story for others who, like me, suffer from depression and low self-esteem. Please know that you are not alone. We are in this together!

First, I would like to thank my husband, Troy McMillian, for believing in me. I love you.

Second, I would like to thank my friend, Shalinie Rohit, for your advice and encouraging words throughout the process. Thank you for being my second pair of eyes and for your insight. You have jumped on this ride with me, and I couldn't imagine doing this without you. I love the friendship we have built over the years; you are amazing!

Third, I would like to thank my author friend and editor, Caron Pescatore. I genuinely love and appreciate you; words are not enough to express how inspiring you have been. I value our friendship, and as I have told you plenty of times, you are indeed God-sent. Thank you!

To my author friend, Billie Jade Kermack, thank you for inspiring me and for all your advice during this process. I truly value our friendship, and I love you.

To my friend Michelle Azizi, thank you so much for all the support you have shown me, from reading and reviewing Bright to being the inspiration behind my fantasy town, Mashalville. I don't know where I would be without you in my life. Thank you for always sticking by my side. I love you!

To Fabiola Cameau, you have been so supportive by sharing my posts, purchasing Bright, and spreading the word to others. Thank you so much; I love you!

To Amy Sobel, girl, you are amazing! Thank you so much for your love and immeasurable support, from our venting sessions to your incredible advice. I can't thank you enough. I love you!

ABOUT THE AUTHOR

When Kiana "K.C." McMillian was a child, she would make up stories in her head and write them down. While attending high school, her favorite play was Romeo and Juliette, and she enjoyed reading it, but she sometimes fumbled over her words while reading in front of her classmates. And, of course, children can be cruel. Kiana didn't like being made fun of and lacked confidence in herself, and she felt that if she couldn't read in front of a crowd, then perhaps she wasn't good enough to write. She didn't think her stories would be well received and feared failing at something she loved. Kiana knew back then that she would one day want to share her imagination with others, but she wasn't sure about putting herself out there.

Fast forward twenty years later, after the death of her husband's grandmother on January 13th, 2022, she decided she wouldn't let the fear of failure hinder her from following her dreams. Before "Gran," as she and her husband called her, left this earth, she said, "I have lived my life, and I've done everything I wanted to do; I'm ready." K.C. knew that if her life suddenly came to a tragic end, she wouldn't be satisfied. That statement inspired her, and she decided to follow her dream of becoming an author.

Printed in Great Britain
by Amazon

23053509R00086